TIC-TAC-MISTLETOE

N.R. WALKER

COPYRIGHT

BLURB

Hamish Kenneally is moving from Australia to the US for a fresh start, beginning with Christmas at his sister's place in Idaho. When a snowstorm diverts his plane to Montana and leaves him stranded two days before Christmas, he hires a car and drives right into a blizzard.

Ren Brooks has always called Hartbridge, Montana, and his family hardware store, home. After a few failed attempts at love, he's resigned to being single forever—after all, no guy wants to stay in his sleepy little town for long. And after his dad's passing earlier in the year, Ren's Christmas is looking bleak. But when a car runs off the road in front of his property, Ren pulls the driver out and takes him home to get out of the cold.

With the storm and the holidays leaving Hamish with nowhere else to go, Ren kindly offers a place to stay. Hamish is certain he's crashed right into a Hallmark Christmas movie, despite more car delays and road closures and the prospect of not seeing his sister for Christmas. And with help from Hamish, Ren is beginning to feel a little Christmas cheer.

These two unlikely strangers have more in common than they first realise, and after two days of Christmas decorations, cookies, and non-stop conversation, it looks like Christmas might be saved after all.

TIC-TAC-
Mistletoe

N.R. WALKER

CHAPTER ONE

HAMISH KENNEALLY

A TOTALLY CATASTROPHIC, unmitigated disaster.

What is a totally catastrophic, unmitigated disaster, you might ask?

Let me break it down for you real quick.

My life, my relationship, my job, my plans, my future, and this whole damn trip.

So, basically me.

Me.

I am the totally catastrophic unmitigated disaster.

Hamish Kenneally, thirty-one-year-old Australian, who quit his shitty job and sold his shitty apartment and left behind his shitty life in Sydney, packed his said-shitty life into two suitcases, and boarded a plane to spend Christmas with his sister in God-knows-where, Idaho, USA.

Well, Christmas first. Then two years, at least, in America trying to unshittify his life.

And if the trip to said God-knows-where, Idaho, was any indication of just how spectacularly extra-shittified my life was going to get, I should have turned around and stayed right where I was.

Because if the flight from Sydney to LA was bad, which it was, then the second flight from LA to Spokane made the first flight look like a joyride.

Because I didn't get to Spokane, did I?

Oh no, of course I didn't.

Because you see, Christmastime in America is in *winter*. Which is weird enough for this Australian. Christmas should be hot summer days at the beach, seafood and salads, beers and watching the bronzed surfers and drunk foreigners at Bondi. That is what Christmas should be.

None of this "sorry folks, to avoid flying into a massive snow blizzard, we're being diverted to Missoula, Montana" crap the captain of the plane said when we were halfway there. Like the screaming baby in the seat next to me, or the vomiting lady in the row in front of me weren't bad enough. Like we had any choice about which direction we were flying into.

I had no choice. I was now going to Montana. In a freaking blizzard, of all things. Ever been on a plane that flew into a snowstorm? There is zero joy in that kind of turbulence, believe me. It would also explain the screaming baby and the vomiting woman. And the man behind me saying Hail Mary's . . . which you'd think might be comforting. But oh boy, is it ever not. Especially when he yelled the prayer every time we hit a particularly large pothole in the sky on the descent. Honestly, if this flight was a scene in a movie, you'd think it was too ridiculous to be real.

After the plane landed—to which I *would* have clapped and cheered like everyone else if I wasn't stuck in the brace position after trying to kiss my own arse goodbye—we were kicked off the plane, without so much as a good luck, in the wrong bloody state.

So there I was, a clueless Aussie, after flying for twenty hellish-hours and now a few hundred kilometres from where I was supposed to be, trying to wrangle two over-weight suitcases down the concourse, when one little wheel on my suitcase broke.

Because of course it did.

Frazzled and trying not to cry— Yes, cry. A thirty-one-year-old man can cry; shove your toxic masculinity in your cakehole and stop judging me. I was having a jetlag-fuelled shitastic day meltdown, trying to keep my shit together the best I could, and clearly not doing it very well. I was allowed a little saltwater leakage.

Anyway, getting back to my story. I tried to call my sister.

No signal.

Because of course there's not.

So, taking a deep breath and willing myself not to spiral, I found my car rental kiosk. *Finally, something is going right.* "I have a car booked," I said, trying to keep my now-broken suitcase upright with my foot while rifling through my back-pack for my booking confirmation and driver's licence. After dropping my passport and half the contents from my backpack all over the floor, then scrambling to collect it all while still trying to keep my suitcase upright, I handed everything over with a flourish of triumph. "Oh, that flight was the worst," I said, sagging onto the counter. I was about to tell her all about my day from the ninth circle of hell when she looked up at me with *that* look.

You know the one.

The look of superficial appeasement before they cut you off at the knees. "I'm sorry, sir. But I don't have a reservation under your name."

I stared at her. My brain short-circuited and the will to

live left my body. It was an actual out-of-body experience, I'm sure of it. I could see myself staring at her, mouth gaping like I'd been lobotomised.

Because of course they didn't have my booking.

Why would they? My rental car was waiting for me in Spokane. In Washington. Not in freaking Montana.

"Oh," I whispered, and my left eye twitched. "That's nice." I looked around the airport, at the line of annoyed people behind me. "Excellent. I've seen that movie where Tom Hanks lives in an airport. It wasn't so bad. Could be worse. Could've been the one where he's stuck on the island, I guess. Though I didn't pack a volleyball, so that would've sucked."

She blinked and tap-tap-tapped away at her keyboard. "But sir, we've had a lot of cancelled flights today because of the weather. I can arrange a vehicle for you, if you'd like?"

Oh, my sweet baby Jesus in a manger, why didn't she lead with that?

"I would like that very much," I said, wiping at my eye with my sleeve. "It's been a day."

She smiled, kindly. "I can see that."

I meant it literally—I left home literally a day ago—but whatever. I checked my phone again. "Uh, are there mobile phone . . . er, cell phone service issues? Or do I need to do some magic overseas-roaming thing to my phone?" I'd asked the phone guy back home what I had to do with my phone and he said—

"Oh, the storm took out a cell tower," she replied. "Could be down a while."

Because *of course* the blizzard took down a cell tower. Because of course it fucking did.

"Oh, I'm supposed to drive to my sister's place," I

added, but then the guy behind me cleared his throat. Clearly my disasters were an inconvenience to him, and I noticed the woman behind him checked her watch. "You know what?" I said, giving the poor woman behind the counter a big ol' smile. "I'll be fine. Who needs a map or directions when you're in a foreign country, huh?"

"Oh, I might have something . . . ," she said, then produced an old fashioned folded map. Like it was 1992. Like they used in the dark ages before the internet. She handed it over, and with a glance to the ever-growing line behind me, I took it.

I signed everything I needed to sign, she spieled off a slew of instructions, and a few minutes later and with a renewed sense of vigour, I was wheeling my wonky suitcases out of the airport.

And directly into the Arctic.

Well, not quite, but close enough. It sure felt like it. The skies were grey, the clouds were low, the wind was a thousand frozen ice needles into my face, and I was cold through to the bone in less than three seconds.

Deciding it was better to find the car instead of freezing to death on the footpath, I followed the signs and pressed the key fob thingy until my car beeped at me. I threw my suitcases in the boot compartment and got into the driver's seat—which was the exact moment I remembered it was on the other side of the car.

Because of course it fucking was.

After getting out and walking around to the other side and getting in behind the actual steering wheel, I took a few deep breaths. I had prepared myself for this. Driving in a different country, on the wrong side of the car, on the wrong side of the road, honestly couldn't be too hard. People did it all the time. And while I might be a totally catastrophic, unmitigated disaster, amongst a long list of other things, contrary to popular belief, I was not an idiot.

I could do this.

I checked my phone, and seeing it had no service, I typed out a quick message to my sister anyway. If, on the off chance there was a tiny blip of service, the message might get through. With that done and with the paper map on the seat beside me, I reversed successfully out of the parking spot. Then, ever so slowly, I drove out of the parking lot. Thankfully there was a line of traffic I could just merge into, and driving on the wrong side of the road wasn't so bad when I was following a line of cars.

I drove a few blocks without a major incident, and I was feeling more and more confident despite the worsening weather out my windscreen. The clouds were lower now, darker too. And the rain had become sleet at some point, and the road was dirty slush. I drove slower than a sedated sloth might have, probably annoying every other driver on the road. I even pulled the car over every few blocks and double-checked on the map that I was on the right road.

Because, you see, I've never driven in sleety, slushy snow before. In actual crazy-fact, I'd never even seen snow before.

Yep, you read that right. Never seen snow before. Never been in snow before, and certainly never driven a car in it. So why on earth did I think my first time should be when I was jet-lagged and driving on the wrong side of the car on the wrong side of the street?

Because I was a grown-ass man and people did this all the time. I was unshittifying my life, taking a leap of faith, starting anew. I had to stand on my own two feet. If my little sister could move across to the other side of the planet and start a new life, then so could I, dammit. I wanted to prove to her—and to myself—that I could be a grown-up.

And driving in Missoula wasn't so bad. There were street signs and freeway signs, and once I was on the Interstate, I was feeling pretty good. It was now actually snowing. White flaky stuff was falling from the sky, not that I had any time to enjoy it. I just concentrated on the red brake lights in front of me and the road signs that confirmed I was heading in the right direction.

But then the signs got fewer and farther between with every kilometre I drove. The line of traffic thinned out to just a few cars, yet the snow was now coming down pretty hard and the only lines on the road I could see were from the tyres of the cars ahead of me.

But I had the map all planned out. All I had to do was stay on the Interstate, get to St. Regis and turn onto Montana Sky Highway. Stay on that until I pass the Welcome to Idaho signs and then take a left on Beaver Creek Road. Take that for another twenty-five miles until I drove right into Mossley, Idaho.

Easy, right?

I could do this.

Yeah, right. Maybe I could do this if ridiculous amounts of white stuff wasn't falling from the sky.

Driving was slow and slippery, the wind making it hard to see the road at times, and drifts of snow crawled onto the highway in some places. I stopped for fuel and the nice guy at the petrol station . . . err, gas station, reassured me I was headed in the right direction. "Just keep going on this road a ways, and you'll see a sign that says Welcome to Idaho. You can't miss it."

I had no idea how far 'a ways' was in metric, but at least I was going in the right direction.

"Still no phone service," I said to him, showing him my phone as if that proved anything.

"Lines are down too," he replied. "Can't even use the landlines."

Well, that's just awesome.

"Haven't seen snow like this since '72," he went on.

Because, of course he hadn't.

The blizzard of the freaking century was the day I turned up and needed to drive in it.

So fucking typical.

I thanked him and wished him a Merry Christmas, then slide-walk-danced back to the car. And from that twenty-metre walk, I still had to brush snow out of my hair and try not to freeze to death.

I double-checked the map—which was ridiculously difficult to fold, mind you. It really is no wonder they went out of fashion. It was like trying to fold a fitted sheet, all while sitting behind the wheel of a car, with frozen fingers.

But, with a renewed confidence that I was actually doing this and that I would see my sister soon, I pulled back out into traffic, and thankfully there was a car in front of me I could follow. But soon enough, they turned off and I was on my own.

Sure, I passed an occasional vehicle going in the other direction, so I wasn't the only one stupid enough to drive in this. But the snow came down heavier now, and driving was slow and difficult. I almost missed the sign for Montana Sky Highway and had to pull a hard right to take the turn. The tyres slid and I almost over-corrected, and thank God there was no one behind me. But my heart was now beating triple time and my hands were shaking. I probably would have hyperventilated if I wasn't concentrating so hard on keeping the car on the damn road.

It took a few kilometres for my heart rate to return to non-cardio-infarction levels, and a few kilometres after that, I realised I was talking to myself. Telling myself I could do this, I was almost there, this was fine, Hamish. This didn't look like some road out of a horror movie at all, and not even serial killers were stupid enough to be out in this stupid weather, and how far did I have to drive on this stupid road? Twenty-five kilometres, right? How far had I driven already?

I let the car come to a crawling stop and double-checked the map, then tried to make sense of what I could see outside my windscreen and the windows . . . but there was nothing. Just trees and so much fucking snow. The road was too narrow for my liking, and I was certain I'd taken the wrong turn somewhere.

I drove the car at a snail's pace, looking for some kind of road sign or mailbox, something with a name or number on it at least.

But there was nothing.

I checked my phone.

Still nothing.

I don't know how long I drove for. I was driving so slow, it was hard to tell. It felt like it took hours but maybe I'd gone just a few kilometres. Or maybe it was ten. And the road was getting harder and harder to see. The snow was making driving close to impossible.

Panic was bubbling up inside me, and now I was really trying not to cry. I was overwhelmed, tired as hell, and so stupid for thinking I could do this, and I was going to die out here, some kind of Australian human popsicle, frozen solid.

And I don't know how it happened. One minute I was

driving on the road, albeit a close-to-panicking mess. The next thing I knew, a corner came up too quick or the tyres didn't stay on the road, or maybe it was the idiot driver who had never driven in snow before, but I was sliding off the road and down a slight embankment.

I think I screamed.

And once the sheer panic and the screaming was over, I realised the engine wasn't going.

I tried the ignition again and . . . nothing.

Oh God, this isn't happening. This isn't happening. Just breathe, Hamish . . .

But this *was* happening! And I was stuck in some wall of snow with no engine, which meant no heating and the snow was still coming down and I could already feel the cold.

So I did the only thing a completely sane person could do. I thumped the horn while I wailed and screamed and lost my shit. "Such. A goddammed. Disaster. Hamish. You. Idiot."

Then, after my screaming and horn-thumping melt-down was over, all those tears that had threatened to fall that I've talked about, well they just built right up in some Moses-worthy flood and spilled out of my eyes.

And so, because I promised myself I wouldn't cry, I thumped the horn again in frustration. Then, once my little dramatic fit was over, I took some deep calming breaths and tried to think of what the bloody hell I was supposed to do now.

God, I was going to have to get out and walk. Were there bears in Montana? Oh my God, there *were* bears in Montana. I'd just had the worst twenty-four hours ever, my life was an on-going shitshow, I ran my car off the road in a freaking blizzard, and now I was going to end up a frozen human popsicle or mauled to death by a bear two days before Christmas.

Then something big and dark and remarkably bear-shaped tapped on my driver's window and scared the ever-loving shite out of me so bad, I let out a high-pitched scream of terror, and I swear to God, I almost peed a little.

CHAPTER TWO

REYNOLD BROOKS

"ARE YOU SURE?" Mrs Barton asked me for perhaps the fifth time today.

"Yes, more than sure."

"I just worry about you being alone for the holidays, is all. And you know we'll have enough food at our place to feed an army. The house will be filled to the rafters, but what's one more? It really would be no problem."

Mrs Peggy Barton had worked three days a week at Hartbridge Hardware for thirty-four years. She was sixty now, with a brood of grandkids she adored, and she really was the sweetest woman I'd ever known. But I knew she wasn't kidding when she said her house would be full to brimming. Her own four kids and their spouses plus the sixteen grandkids and a great-aunt from the nursing home, was a little *too* full to brimming for me. I wasn't up for that kind of family holiday.

Not this year, anyway.

"I really appreciate the offer, Mrs Barton," I said. "But I'm fine, thank you. And I won't be alone. I have Chutney."

We both turned to look at my dog Chutney who was

laying by the service counter. She tilted her head at her name, the cute way dogs do, and Mrs Barton turned back to me and sighed. "Are you sure you'll be okay?"

"I'll be fine," I reassured her. Again. "Now, you better get going before this storm hits."

"Yes, yes," she said as she pulled on her overcoat. "And you should too. It's really starting to come down now. Don't stay late today, promise?"

"I promise," I said, smiling.

And she was right. There was a storm rolling in from the east, and it was supposed to dump a few feet of snow overnight. It was midday, December twenty-third and it was already getting dark and gloomy outside. Snow had been falling pretty steadily all morning, and all the last-minute Christmas shoppers had left Main Street an hour ago. Hell, my last customer was about an hour before that.

It had been a busy week though, with everyone getting their homes ready for Christmas, fixing things around the house before guests arrived. And vacation time was a good excuse to do those chores they'd be putting off all year. The holidays were always a busy time of year in the hardware business.

I followed Mrs Barton to the front door and made sure she got her car started okay. I waved her off as she drove away and glanced down the snow-covered street. It was empty; not a car or a customer in sight. Main Street, Hartbridge, didn't have much exactly: a hair salon, convenience store, electronics store, auto shop, library, a few clothes stores, and town hall.

Hartbridge's one and only diner, which was directly across from my hardware store, was still open, though I doubted they'd be open for long. I took out my phone to put a lunch order in, but there was still no service.

Dammit.

I threw on my coat, pulled on my knitted hat, and went out the front door. I didn't even lock the door. The good folks of Hartbridge were as honest as the day was long, but there was no one around for miles. I could see if anyone drove up anyway and be back in the store in just a few seconds.

The diner was warm, and pulling off my hat, I smiled at Carl who came out to see who had made the front door chime. He was a middle-aged man, kinda round in the middle, and he made the best homemade pie in the state. "Ah, Ren," he said, smiling. He nodded to the front windows. "Looks like it's settling in out there."

"Yep. Gonna be a good storm, I'd say. Think you'll be open for long?"

"Nope. Was just clearing out the fridges now. I saw McGee pull his shutters down about an hour ago."

McGee was the mechanic down the road. "Not many folks out driving in this weather," I replied.

"Nah, suppose not. What can I get for you? Did you want something to take home? You know, I think I have some of that berry cobbler you like."

"You know me too well." I grinned at him. "Have you got any of that roast beef left over from lunch yesterday?"

"Sure do! Let me go see what I can find."

He disappeared back through the swinging doors into the kitchen and I turned to the front windows, watching the snow in front of my shop. Hartbridge Hardware had been there for almost seventy years now. My grandfather's boss had started the store way back then and sold it to my grandfather, who passed it on to his son, my dad.

And now it was mine.

I grew up in that store. I knew every grain in those

wooden floors; I knew every bolt and screw, every pipe, every creak in the stairs. My earliest memories are of being in there with my dad, sitting up on the counter, all of four years old. I stacked shelves when I was not much older than that and worked there after school and on weekends.

And still, every morning when I'd unlock the doors and flip on the lights, that familiar smell made me smile.

It smelled of love and hard work. It smelled like my dad . . .

"Here you go, Ren," Carl said, startling me. He slid three takeout containers onto the counter and pointed to each in turn as he put them into a bag. "Pie. Roast beef, baked veggies, and gravy for you. And some roast offcuts for little Chutney."

And that was just one of the reasons I loved this town. "Aw, Carl, you are a Christmas angel."

He beamed at that. "Say, who are you spending Christmas with this year?"

"Just me and Chutney," I said, knowing where this was going.

"You come and have dinner with us," he said. "You know my Jenny would love to see you for the holidays."

"I'm okay," I said gently. "But thank you. It's a very kind offer, but I'll be fine. You enjoy your Christmas." I took the bag and slid a twenty onto the counter. "And let someone else do the cooking for a change. Have a day off."

"I have two pies to make tomorrow," he said, and we both knew it was no chore. He loved every minute.

"Give everyone my best," I said, heading back out into the cold.

"Be good!" he called out, and I heard him lock the door behind me. I made it back into my store and turned the sign from open to closed, then slid home the deadbolt. I pulled the shutters down and Chutney was soon under my feet, very interested in the bag of food I had.

"Soon, girl," I said, giving her a quick rub on the head. "Let's get home, huh?"

After everything was done, I pulled the back door locked and got Chutney and the bag of food into my truck and cranked the heat on, ready for three days off work. Three days of quiet, three days of watching movies, reading books, making soup, and pretending I wasn't lonely.

And truth be told, I wasn't lonely. Well, for 362 days of the year I wasn't. But Thanksgiving, Christmas, and my birthday were the worst. I loved my life in Hartbridge. I'd spent time in Denver and even LA, but I was a country boy at heart.

I was a *gay* country boy, which seemed to add to my loneliness. Not that the good folks of Hartbridge had a problem with it. There just wasn't a line of eligible gay guys knocking on my door. Hell, there weren't any gay guys, eligible or not.

Most of the kids who grew up in Hartbridge couldn't wait to leave, but the LGBTQ kids? They were gone as soon as they were able. I didn't blame them. They needed more than what this town had to offer, and I got that. But my heart was here. I couldn't leave, even if I wanted to. I'd long ago made peace with a possible life of solitude, and I didn't even miss sex that much. After a while, it wasn't important.

Chutney yipped at me, probably wondering why we were still parked behind the shop and why I was staring out the windshield at the still-falling snow and not driving home already.

"Yeah, okay," I grumbled. "I know you can smell what's in that bag."

Chutney grinned at me, so I gave her another quick pat, put the truck into gear, and made the slow drive home.

TRUE TO FORM, Carl had given me enough food to feed both me and Chutney for three days. Once we'd eaten enough, I stoked up the fire and decided I should cart some more wood up from the woodpile to the porch so it could dry over the next few days. The storm was coming in hard now and it'd be a few days before anyone was going anywhere. I had enough dry wood to last me a few weeks if needed, but I'd always been told it was best to be prepared for the worst.

I pulled on my coat and hat, snow boots and gloves, and went out to the side of the house and trudged through the snow toward the woodshed when I heard something. The snow and wind could play tricks with your mind, making you think you hear things that aren't there, but I could have sworn there was a faint noise coming from the road.

I stopped and listened, hearing it again. I pulled off my hat and turned my ear to the sound.

A car horn.

Someone was in trouble.

I pulled my hat back on and ran to the house to grab my keys, then raced back to my truck with Chutney on my heels. I turned the engine over and she rumbled to life. I threw her into first gear and we took off down the drive.

I'd heard the sound on the right side of my house so I turned that way, and sure enough, just a few hundred yards up the road I could see some red brake lights through the white of the snow.

A car had run off the road.

I pulled up behind them and jumped out, leaving Chutney in the truck. I raced up to the driver's side and knocked on the window, making the driver scream.

Panicking now that something was terribly wrong, I opened their door. "Are you okay?"

A man put his hands up, terrified and a little hysterical. "I'm too pretty to be bear poo!"

I stopped, trying to get his words to make sense. "Huh?"

He looked at me, then, from behind his hands. "Oh my God. You're not a grizzly bear?"

"Not the last time I checked," I replied. "Sir, are you okay?"

Then he put his face into his hands. "It's been the worst day ever." He mumbled something else about some disaster. He had blackish hair, pale white skin with a bit of a dark beard, and when he looked up at me, I saw the brownest eyes I'd ever seen. "My car won't go."

Clearly there was nothing broken or bleeding; he wasn't in any pain; he didn't seem to have hit his head. "You need to get out of the vehicle," I said. "Can you walk?"

He nodded and then proceeded to fumble with the seatbelt. He wasn't wearing gloves. Actually, he wasn't wearing any weather-appropriate clothes. Sweet mercy, the jacket he was wearing was no thicker than a shirt.

"Are you a serial killer? I really hope you're not a serial killer, though to be honest, I'd probably just roll with it at this point."

Was he for real?

"Not a serial killer," I replied. He had an accent though. "Come on." I helped him out of his car. He was shivering and I could tell he'd been crying. "Let's get you into my truck." He looked concerned, and probably rightfully so.

He'd just been in an accident, but he needed to move. "Or you can stand here and freeze to death."

He moved then and I ushered him to my truck and opened the door for him. He climbed up, shaking and shivering. "M-m-my bags. In the boot."

"The boot?"

"T-t-runk."

I was going to say to hell with his bags, but I had to go back and secure his car anyway. I ran back and took the keys out of the ignition, and seeing his phone in the console and a backpack on the passenger seat, I grabbed them before locking the doors. Pocketing the phone, I popped the trunk and wrestled the two suitcases out and threw them into the bed of my truck and climbed into the warmth of the cab.

To find Chutney perched up on the guy's lap. He was still shivering and he was sitting on his hands, probably trying to keep them warm. "Uh, your d-d-dog just did this. I didn't a-a-ask him to, he just s-s-sat on me. I'm sorry."

I patted the seat between us. "Chutney, here."

Chutney refused to move, which wasn't like her at all. Jeez, maybe she could recognise near hypothermia and was trying to transfer some of her tiny body heat. "Okay, let's get you somewhere warm," I said. Putting the truck into first, I slowly turned us around and headed for home.

"What a-about my car?" he asked.

"We'll worry about that in a bit," I replied. "It's off the road so no one will hit it."

He nodded, still shaking. When I turned into my drive, he looked at me. "W-where are you taking me?"

"To my house." I pointed up ahead. My driveway was a quarter-mile long. "You're lucky I heard you."

"Heard me?"

"Your car horn. I just went outside for a quick minute. Thirty seconds later and I wouldn't have heard you at all."

He lifted his gloveless hand to his forehead. "Oh. Thank you. I don't know what I would have done . . ."

I pulled up by the house, just needing to get him inside before he caught his death. I jumped out and went to his door and he was still shaking so much I had to help him get down. I led him up the stairs and ushered him inside, sitting him by the fire. I pulled the throw off the back of the couch and wrapped it around his shoulders. "Stay here. I'll be right back."

He nodded, and Chutney stayed by his side while I went back out into the snowstorm. I grabbed his gear and dumped it on the porch, then drove the truck into the garage before jogging back and taking his bags inside.

He hadn't moved, if shivering didn't count. He was going to rattle the teeth out of his head.

"Feeling any warmer?" I asked, pulling my gloves off. I hung my coat up by the door.

He was shivering too hard to answer. I went to him and knelt down at his feet, feeling his jeans. They weren't too wet, but his feet were. "I'm going to take your shoes and socks off," I said. He nodded again and Chutney jumped up onto his lap. His shoes were some high-end brand sneaker and his socks were just standard thin cotton. Jesus. "I'm going to guess you're not from around here."

"Sydney," he replied. "Australia. When I left it was thirty-five degrees. Celsius, that is. Like ninety-something for you. I don't know. It's summer."

I wondered where the accent was from. "You left Sydney today?"

He nodded. "Well, yesterday. I guess. It's been a long day. And terrible flights—oh my God—like you couldn't believe. I haven't slept. Can't sleep on a plane. Your dog is really cute. I think he likes me. What's his name?"

I smiled up at them, given Chutney was on his lap smiling back at me. "She's a she. Her name is Chutney."

"Chutney," he repeated. "That's just the cutest."

"She's a Cavoodle, or Cavapoo, or Cavadoodle, I don't know. Some hybrid name. She's half Cavalier, half poodle, one hundred per cent spoiled rotten."

"The poodle half explains the black curly hair." His dark eyes met mine and he smiled. "Oh my God. Chutney? From *Legally Blonde*?"

I smiled because he knew. No one here got the reference, certainly no guys. "Yep. I love that movie." Feeling my cheeks heat a little, I stood up. "I'll be back in one second. Put your hands near the fire."

I came back with a pair of wool socks and exchanged the socks for my dog. "Put these on. I'm going to make you something warm to drink," I explained. "It'll help warm you up from the inside. Hot chocolate okay?"

"Uh, sounds perfect, actually."

I left him to put on the socks, and by the time I'd heated milk on the stove and handed him a cup, he'd stopped shivering. "Oh, and this," I said, remembering his phone in my pocket. "It was in your car."

He tapped the screen but frowned at it. "There's still no service."

"Probably won't be for a bit. Happens in these kinds of storms," I explained. "You feeling better?" I asked, sitting on the sofa opposite him.

He smiled and nodded. "I am, thank you." He sipped the hot chocolate and hummed. "I can't imagine what would have happened if you hadn't saved me."

I smiled at him over the top of my cup. "You probably would have frozen to death in your car."

He nodded again but he frowned this time. "I was supposed to fly into Spokane," he added. "I'm going to see my sister for Christmas. Oh, she's going to be so worried. And my car . . . well, the rental car. I slid off the road into more snow and it wouldn't start. I'll need to call someone about that too, I guess. I don't even know where I am. I think I took a wrong turn."

"You're about five miles outside of Hartbridge, Montana."

"I'm still in *Montana*? But I drove for ages."

I couldn't help but chuckle. "You haven't driven in snow very often, have you?"

"Driven in it? I'd never even *seen* snow before today."

My smile died because that wasn't funny. "Never seen . . ."

He shook his head. "In movies and stuff, sure. But not in real life."

Oh, dear Lord. I couldn't believe it. He'd never even seen snow before! That certainly explained his clothing choice and lack of preparedness. He seriously could have died out there if he'd gotten out of the car to try to find help. "But you feel okay now," I said, sipping my hot chocolate.

"Much better. The fire is lovely. The socks are great, thank you." He made a face and chewed on his lip for a bit. "I'm embarrassed, to be honest. I was trying to go by some foldable map the car rental lady gave me. I must have taken the wrong turn, and then the car wouldn't start. I had these visions of being eaten by a bear."

"A bear?"

"Yes! You have those here, right?"

"Uh, sure. But it's winter and they hibernate."

"Oh, thank fu—" He baulked. "I mean, thank goodness for that."

I chuckled, remembering what he'd said about being too pretty to be bear poo when I opened his car door. "You thought I was a bear?"

"Your coat was brown and your hat was brown, your gloves were black," he said. "It was snowing and I couldn't see because I was crying because my life is a bit of a mess—just gonna put that out there from the get-go. And I'm jet-lagged to hell and I thought it'd be a great idea to drive to my sister's place, but the plane was diverted to the wrong state. In a car where the steering wheel is on the wrong side, and you all drive on the wrong side of the road, mind you. In a freaking blizzard, no less. Where running the car off the road is just a cherry on a very big pile of steaming . . ." He paused. "Not-cake."

I smiled at him, the way he rambled, the way the tips of his ears went red, the way he chewed on his bottom lip. I'd always thought it'd be a miracle should some cute guy ever walk into my life, but maybe he didn't walk. Maybe he ran his car off the road and almost froze to death instead. And I didn't even know his name.

"My name's Reynold Brooks, by the way," I said. "People around here call me Ren."

He stared at me for a long moment; his lips played with a smile. "Nice to meet you, Ren. I'm Hamish Kenneally."

I don't know why, but hearing him say his own name woke some butterflies in my belly. "Well, Hamish. It's nice to meet you too."

CHAPTER THREE

HAMISH

WHEN I STOPPED SHIVERING and could finally breathe properly, I could appreciate Ren a whole lot more. Don't get me wrong, I appreciated him when he pulled me out of my car, stuffed me into his truck, then all but carried me into his house. I appreciated the thick socks and the hot chocolate too; don't misunderstand.

I mean *appreciate*.

He was taller than my five ten by a good few inches. He had blue eyes, sandy brown hair, short and kinda messy from his beanie. He had big hands, working hands, rough and strong. He wore a blue flannel shirt and long work pants with heavy boots. He had a lumberjack vibe going on, and not some faux look the city boys tried to aim for. He was the real deal.

His house was a big log cabin from what I could see of the one room I'd been in. I'd been alert enough to notice the wrap-around veranda out the front and some sheds and outbuildings by the side of the house when we'd driven up. His place was surrounded by trees, and I was fairly certain

I'd managed to run the car off the road in the exact middle of nowhere.

Well, a few miles outside of Hartbridge, Montana, apparently. Wherever the hell that was.

And as far as the serial-killer thing went, the location was probably right. But I was guessing serial killers didn't make hot chocolate and give their victims fluffy socks. That'd be traceable evidence, right? I really should broach that subject again.

"Uh, I'm sorry for asking if you were serial killer as well. That was probably rude. But you said no, right?"

Ren chuckled and drained the last of his hot chocolate. "Yeah, I said no."

"Well, that's a relief," I replied. "Not that I'd suspect a serial killer to just straight up admit it, but I'm guessing serial killers don't name their dogs after characters from *Legally Blonde*."

He aimed a smile right at me. "And I'm guessing serial killers wouldn't get the reference to *Legally Blonde*, so you're not a serial killer either, right?"

I put his hand to my chest, horrified. "Me? I can't even kill spiders and blood makes me squeamish, so that's a definite no. Plus, how would I overpower anyone so I could actually kill them? I have the upper body strength of wet paper."

He laughed at that, the sound warm and rumbly. "Well, I'm glad we've established neither of us are serial killers."

And I don't know if it was the relief, the warm fire, the hot chocolate, or the fluffy socks, but I was so tired I couldn't stifle a yawn. "I'm sorry, I've been awake for far too long and I've taken up enough of your time. If I could call a tow truck for the car, that'd be great."

"Well, actually you can't."

What? I can't use his phone? Is he . . . ? "Oh. But you said you're not a serial killer, and—"

He laughed again. "No, the phone lines are down. And honestly, Hamish, this storm is set in and it's getting dark out. I don't think you should be driving at night, even if we could get your car out."

But . . . but . . . "Where am I supposed to stay? Is there a hotel in Hartbridge?"

He made a face. "There's a motel, but they were closed when I left town. Had the no-vacancy sign up, and I can't even call them to ask for you."

"Can I email them? Do emails even work?" Oh God. "How can I call a taxi? Or Uber? My sister is going to start calling the police, thinking I'm missing or dead. I called her when I landed in LA. She was so excited. I haven't seen her in four years." I let my head fall back onto the couch, every hour of missed sleep now settling inside my bones. "Everything is such a disaster."

"I have a spare bedroom," Ren said quietly. Then he cleared his throat. "I have two spare rooms, actually. It's not what you're probably used to, coming from a city and all. But it's warm and dry, and you can barely keep your eyes open." He stood up and took my empty mug and walked into the kitchen. "I have a CB radio. I can put a call in for your car, and they'll tow it as soon as they're able. And I can notify the local sheriff. See if he can get word to your sister."

I stood up, keeping the blanket around my shoulders, and found Ren leaning against the kitchen cupboard, arms crossed and trying to be casual. "You'd do that?" I asked.

He ran his hand over his face and nodded to the kitchen window. All I could see was white. "No one's going anywhere right now, and you're just about dead on your feet. We'll see what it looks like outside come morning."

I was so grateful and so damn tired, I could have cried. "Thank you."

He smiled, real brief and real beautiful. "You're welcome. There's a shower too, if you've been travelling all day. Might make you feel better."

"I do feel kinda gross," I admitted. "Being on planes and in airports leaves you grimy, you know?"

Ren shrugged. "Well, no. I've never been on a plane before. Or even in an airport."

Now it was my turn to stare at him. "Never?"

He shook his head sadly. "Nope."

"Wow. Does my expression match your 'you've never seen snow?' face?"

That earned me a bit of a smile. "I've travelled a bit here. Spent some time in LA and I've been to Canada. It's just up the road, really." He shrugged. "But this is my home. Not just this house. Hartbridge, I mean. This town is my home."

"You're lucky," I murmured. "Having a place where you know you belong."

He met my gaze, eyes flashing with something I couldn't quite read. "You don't have that back in Sydney?"

I shook my head. "I'm here in the States for two years. My sister is here and I was kinda lost back home, so she suggested I come visit and see how I liked it."

"Lost?"

"Just . . . floundering. I dunno how to explain it. Like you said, you know this town is your home. Well, I'm the opposite of that. I never felt at home there. I wasn't happy, so I quit my job, sold my apartment, and here I am." I shrugged. "Only, now I managed to get myself lost here too."

He smiled at that but there was almost a sadness to it. "Well, I hope you find what you're looking for."

"Me too." I hadn't meant for our conversation to get so deep, so I took a deep breath and changed the subject with a smile. "So, Ren Brooks, what is it that you do?"

His smile was more genuine now. "I have the hardware store in town."

"You do? That's awesome. I feel like I landed in a Hallmark movie or something. Scenic mountains, small town, snowstorm, rescued by the handsome stranger who also happens to have the local hardware store. I should totally sell them my story."

Ren laughed, his cheeks flushed a little. "Well, this town is as pretty as you'll ever see, but I don't know about a handsome stranger."

"No, believe me. Every Hallmark movie has one."

He sighed. "Never really was a fan of those movies, to be honest."

"Neither. Christmas in winter is odd to me."

"Ah." His face lit up. "So this will be your first white Christmas."

"Well, yeah. If I ever get to my sister's place." Then I looked out the window. "I always thought there was something magical about snow, but now I've actually seen it, I'm not so sure."

"There is," Ren said. "Something magical about it. The first snow of the season is always special. And the last. It means spring is around the corner."

I couldn't fight the yawn that had been trying to escape. "Sorry. I'm knackered."

He took pity on me. "How about we take your bags to the spare room. Have a shower and I'll see if I can get the old CB radio working. I'll put a call into McGee's. He's the local mechanic and tow truck driver for your car. And I can see if Ronny can get a message to your sister."

"Ronny?"

"Oh, he's the local sheriff, sorry." Ren walked to my bags still by the front door. "Here, I'll help you carry these."

There was water on the floor from my luggage. "Shit, I didn't realise they were that wet from the snow." I grabbed a tea towel from the kitchen counter. "I'll just mop that up."

"Don't worry too much. I can get that. Most of it's probably from my boots anyway."

I dabbed the puddles anyway, desperately trying not to make a wet spot joke. My brain lacked a filter on a good day, especially when I was tired, but it was all but absent if I was jet-lagged. "There, all dried," I said, rubbing the towel over the luggage as well. I stood up, not realising just how close I was to him. I folded the sodden tea towel, making a face at the squelch and dripping water. "'No, no. Ew, David,'" I said, running it back to the sink.

Ren laughed, and when I turned back to look at him, he was still smiling. "*Schitt's Creek* fan?"

I grinned at him. "Love it."

"Same." He stared at me, just smiling and not speaking. Until he seemed to realise and made a point of picking up one suitcase. "Right, okay. Spare room."

"One of them has a wonky wheel. It broke today," I said, quickly collecting the other suitcase and my backpack. "When I was trying to not have a meltdown in the middle of the wrong airport in the wrong state at the wrong car rental kiosk."

His smile softened. "You've had a day, haven't you?"

"I sure have. But it's gotten considerably brighter, I have to say. Thank you, again, for putting me up for the night. I really do appreciate it."

"You're welcome." He led the way down a short hall and opened a door. He flicked on the light switch and put the suitcase down by the foot of the bed. The room was rustic and cute. There was a double bed with a green quilted cover, a chest of drawers, and framed vintage pictures of trout on the wall. It was very country, very male, and very lovely.

"This is great, thanks," I said, not realising he'd gone.

He appeared just a second later with two folded towels. "Yeah, it's . . . uh . . . I saw pictures in a fancy magazine of a country cabin all done up and fancy. I copied it." He shrugged. "Well, kind of. But I like how it turned out."

I smiled at his honesty. "You know, when interior decorators do that, it's not called copying. They call it using it as 'inspiration,'" I said, using finger quotes.

He chuckled. "Well, they *inspired* all three bedrooms." He rocked back on his heels as if he was nervous for some reason. "It's a bit cold in here right now but it'll warm up with the door open. I'll go and check the old CB radio before it gets too late. Bathroom's across the hall."

He disappeared and I stood there, feeling weird, if I was being honest. I was not where I was supposed to be; I'd had a spectacularly long and shitty day. I was in some random stranger's house, in a strange country. Yet I felt welcome and like I was no bother at all. Kind of like being lost and overwhelmed but being safe and relaxed at the same time. And that was weird.

Maybe I was jet-lagged beyond reason.

That hot shower sounded too good to delay another minute, so opening up my suitcase, I found some comfy track pants and a long-sleeved shirt and my bag of toiletries and went across the hall.

The bathroom had been updated recently by my guess.

New white subway tiles on the walls, dark grey on the floor, a matching vanity, and a simple mirror. All the taps and faucets were a matte black industrial style and the towel rack was matching black industrial pipe, which was very cool and not what I expected at all. But then I remembered that Ren ran the local hardware store, so it kind of made sense.

He was intriguing, that was for sure. Not to mention gorgeous. I wasn't kidding when I said my meeting him was straight out of a Hallmark movie. He was country-rugged and charming, polite and generous, had the cutest accent I'd ever heard, and the bluest eyes . . .

I definitely got a gay vibe from Ren. Not that I could ever be certain. Not like me . . . People knew I was gay the second I opened my mouth or waved my hand around. I'd always leaned to the feminine side, despite my beard. But Ren was definitely a man's man, and if he were in a gay bar, he'd be labelled a cub or even a bear, given he looked to be in his early thirties. But his gaze lingered a touch longer than a straight guy's normally would, and not forgetting he named his dog after *Legally Blonde*, and he loved *Schitt's Creek*. Not that one needed to be gay to like either of these things, but a single guy living by himself in the middle of nowhere? Wouldn't a straight guy name his dog after . . . well, I had no idea what a straight guy would call his dog. I didn't know many straight guys to pass stereotypical judgement.

Wait. Was he single? Why was I presuming that? Why was I interested?

There was a very good chance I'd be leaving tomorrow and would never see him again.

And that would be a shame. I wanted to know more about him. I didn't know why, or what it was about him that intrigued me, but as I scrubbed the grime of the day away and changed into my comfy clothes, I was determined to find out.

I dumped my dirty clothes in my room and took his fluffy socks back out to the living room. Chutney was asleep by the fire. Ren wasn't there but I could hear him talking and what sounded like a whole bunch of static. "No, no injuries. He's fine. Over . . . A sedan, four-door. About halfway between my place and Tucker's driveway. Over . . . Thank you. Over . . ."

I pulled the socks on and followed the sound of his voice. Through the kitchen there was a doorway into what looked like a mudroom. There was a chest freezer in the corner, a built-in stand thing with a rack for coats and hats and a bench seat with a spot for boots underneath. There was also an old cabinet that Ren was leaning on with a CB radio like the truck drivers use. He smiled when I walked in and hung up the receiver. "McGee's are on their way to pull your car out."

"Now? What time is it?" I turned to the windows on the back wall. If I looked past the snow sticking to the windows, it was pretty dark out.

Ren nodded. "It's four o'clock."

"God. It feels like midnight."

He smiled. "Feel better after a shower?"

"So much better, thank you. I almost feel human."

"You must be tired."

"Yeah, but I probably should go change again if the tow truck guys are coming."

"They'll be towing it back to the shop. I told them it wouldn't start." Then he frowned. "I can ask him to drop it off here if you'd prefer. Sorry, I should have asked."

"Uh, no, the shop is fine. I'll need them to fix it or the

rental company can get me another one, or something. I don't know how that works, to be honest. I need to read over the fine print again."

"Okay, so did you want me to see if Ronny can get a message to your sister?"

"Oh yes, please. She's probably beside herself."

Ren put his big warm hand on my shoulder. "So where does she live?"

"Mossley, Idaho. 164 Fairbrook Road."

"Her name?"

"Oh, sorry. Olivia Hampton. She lives with her husband. His name is Josh Hampton, if that helps."

Ren nodded and picked up the little hand receiver again. "He should be on this channel," Ren said, then pressed the button on the side. "Baker County Sheriff, come in. Baker County Sheriff office, come in. Over."

There was a lot of static but after a few seconds, a voice cut in. "This is the Sheriff's office. Over."

"Hey Ronny, it's Reynold Brooks here. I know you're probably busy with the lines down and all but I have a communication request. It's *not* life-threatening. Over."

"Ren, good to hear from you, son. Don't normally do communication requests. What's the problem? Over."

"I have a guy here who was travelling through and his car ran off the road. He's fine, Ronny. There are no injuries, and McGee's are taking his car so I said he could stay here at my place. But he was supposed to be arriving at his sister's in Mossley, and we have no way of letting her know he's okay. He's arrived from Australia today and she's expecting him, so she must be worried sick. I was wondering if you could let the Mossley police know and they might be so kind as to let her know. Over."

There was a beat of silence. "You said he's not injured? Over."

"No, no injuries. Over."

"Well, good. Are you safe, Ren? You shouldn't be letting no strangers into your home, son. If you want me to drive out and bring him back here, I've got a holding cell that'll do just fine. Over."

I blanched at that and Ren laughed. "No, it's all good, Ronny. I'm more than capable of looking after myself. Over." He rolled his eyes.

"Yeah, I know. Just pays to be careful, okay? Now, have you got a name and address and a telephone number for this sister of his? Over."

I dashed back to grab my phone, and when I got back, he'd finished giving the name and address. I found Liv's number and handed over my phone so Ren could read it directly.

"I can't make any promises, but I'll see what I can do," Ronny said. "They're working to restore phone lines, but this storm should move out by tomorrow anyhow, just in time for Christmas . . . Say, speaking of, you have yourself a Merry Christmas, Ren. This time of year probably won't be easy, and especially now your dad's gone. Poker nights just aren't the same without him. So you take care, and if I hear anything from the sister in Mossley, I'll be in touch. Over."

Ren's smile was gone, his shoulders seemed a little lower. *Oh man.* "You too, Ronny," he replied, his voice quieter. "Have a Merry Christmas. Give Geraldine my best. Over." He replaced the hand receiver in its cradle and tried to smile. "Hopefully they can let your sister know."

"Thank you," I offered gently, trying to read his expression. He was guarded and trying to be polite, this kind stranger who had obviously not long ago lost his father. I wasn't sure what I could say, given I didn't know him, only that he'd been incredibly generous and welcoming. "I really do appreciate everything you've done for me."

His smile brightened, though it was still twinged with sadness. "You hungry?"

"Um . . . I suppose." I shrugged. "I'm so tired, I don't know what I am. But I'm trying not to fall asleep just yet or I'll be awake at 3:ooam."

"A belly full of food will help you sleep."

"True." I turned to the back windows, to the snow falling and swirling, made even prettier by the fading daylight. "I can't believe this is normal for you."

That made him smile. "What's winter like for you?"

"Back in Sydney? Windy and cold, with temperatures that would probably be a summer day for you."

"No snow?"

"Nope. A bit like LA, I guess."

He nodded as though that made sense, then walked back to the kitchen and waited for me to follow before closing the door behind us. "So, you're here for two years, huh?"

"Yeah. Well, that's what my visa says. My sister came for two years, loved it, and stayed. That was four years ago."

"You haven't seen her in four years?"

I shook my head. "Nope. We do FaceTime and Zoom chats. But not in person."

He took some containers out of the fridge and sat them on the counter. "I'm sorry you couldn't see her today."

Now it was my turn for sad smiles. "Me too."

"Mossley is about forty miles from here," Ren said, taking a plate from an overhead cupboard. He set about dishing up some kind of roasted meat and veggies. "Roast beef okay?"

"Perfect."

"I think you might have turned off the main road about fifteen miles too soon. If you'd have kept going, there are signs to Idaho not far along. That road takes you down to Mossley. The turn you took came back south. But it's not that far at all."

"So close but yet so far."

He put the plate in the microwave, tidied up, then proceeded to set the table. God, the man had more manners and etiquette than all the men I'd dated combined, which wouldn't exactly be difficult, but still, it was such a nice change.

"With a bit of luck McGee's can get your car out and fix whatever's wrong with it," he said as he busied himself with cutlery and a placemat. "And you can get to see your sister tomorrow. I don't know much about new model cars. I know enough about my truck to keep her running, but she's old and I've had her forever. Newer cars are a different language."

"I know how to put petrol in one," I offered. "Or gas, I should say. Guess I'm gonna have to get used to saying American things now."

He chuckled. "Or not. Keep the Australian. I like it." He turned to the cupboard and took out a glass, then grabbed a jug of water from the fridge so I couldn't see his face. But was he blushing?

"I really like your home," I said after a beat, not wanting things to get awkward. "And I say home and not house because it feels like a home."

"Thanks," he said, taking the plate out of the microwave and putting it on the placemat. He pulled out the chair and smiled at me, waiting.

Jesus. He pulled my seat out.

I sat, and only then did he sit opposite me. "Are you not eating?"

"I ate just a few hours ago, when I got home. Had a short day today. The main street was a ghost town today because of the storm."

I took a forkful of the beef and some roast potato. "Oh wow. Did you cook this?"

He shook his head, smiling. "No. Carl's diner is across the road from my store. I asked for one lunch and he gave me enough for three. He even gave me a container just for Chutney."

"Do you know everyone in Hartbridge by their first name?"

"Yeah, pretty much." He frowned. "Is that . . . lame?"

I had to swallow my mouthful of food to answer quickly. "No, the opposite, actually. I think it's great. Where I'm from, I didn't even know my neighbours' names. Well, there was a Simon in the apartment next to mine and I only know that because his girlfriend used to call it out when the headboard was banging against the wall."

Ren laughed. "No way."

"Yes way. Most nights. It was terrible."

"I bet it was . . . Well, not for Simon."

I chuckled as I took a sip of water. "My apartment wasn't too bad, and it wasn't so much Sydney or my old job. It was just everything. It felt like it was all closing in around me. And being in the city, surrounded by people and every-thing moving fast around me and being alone and stagnant is the worst feeling." I shook my head, not really sure why I dumped all that on Ren. I definitely needed sleep. "But I left that all behind, and here I am."

"It's incredibly brave."

"Or incredibly reckless. As quite a few people told me before I left."

He shook his head slowly. "Brave."

"Well, not too brave. I had a meltdown on day one, so there's that. Oh, and I thought you were a bear. Not sure what kind of bear would tap nicely on a window . . ."

"A polite one."

I laughed. "True."

"So what did you do for work back home?"

"Corporate finance insurance."

He grimaced.

I nodded. "Yep. Every colleague my age was either married with kids or a coke addict. Burnt out by their forties. It was time for me to get out."

"How old are you? If you don't mind me asking."

"Thirty-one."

"I'm thirty-two," he volunteered. "It's . . ." He shook his head, not finishing his sentence. He gently scratched the table, staring at it. "I'll spend my life here, and I'm okay with that. I'm no high-flyer or anything like that. Just want a simple life." He frowned again. "Hartbridge is a great town where everyone knows everyone. I'm the third-generation Brooks to own the hardware store, so it's in my blood."

Third generation? "Wow."

He met my gaze and nodded. "Yep. My granddaddy, then my dad, and now me." He stared at the table again, seeing things only he could see, and it was clear he wasn't done talking, so I gave him the time he needed. "It could have turned out so different for me here, and I know some kids didn't have it so easy. Growing up here, being expected to work the family business, settle down and marry a nice girl . . ." He shook his head. "I uh . . . that wasn't, um . . ."

He was trying to say it but just wasn't quite able to get the words out.

"Or marry a nice boy," I offered with a shrug, aiming for nonchalant. I stabbed a slice of roast pumpkin. "If you wanted to, that is."

He let out a relieved breath and his cheeks tinted pink. He smiled at me and a mutual recognition passed between us. Like I said, most people knew I was gay the second I spoke, so he wasn't just putting out feelers to confirm my gayness. He was testing the waters to admit his own.

"And people in this town are okay with that," he said. "With me not wanting to marry a girl. I owe that to my dad. I told him in my senior year, but I bet he knew already. Folks in town had started to talk, you know. I wasn't interested in girls but I could watch hockey and football players all day long." I laughed at that and he smiled. "Anyway, he told everyone in town there was nothing wrong with having a gay kid, and everyone in town liked my dad. So him acting like it was no big deal made it no big deal, and by the time I left high school, no one cared. I was just the same old Ren who'd been working in the store since I could walk."

"I love that."

He met my eyes. "There aren't any secrets in Hartbridge. Everyone knows everybody's business, but everyone looks out for one another. It's what we do." He swallowed hard and licked his lips. "My dad passed away back in February, and this whole town supported me. Just today I had three invites for Christmas dinner because they were worried I'll be alone. You know, first Christmas without my dad here . . ."

"I'm really sorry to hear that," I whispered. "You sounded very close."

"We were. It was only ever him and me. My mother

bailed on us when I was about two. I don't remember her. My dad raised me." His smile was so sad it made my heart ache. "The hardware store was my second home when I was growing up. Before school, after school, weekends." He met my gaze. "He was a good man."

I reached out and squeezed his hand, just for a moment, before letting go. "I understand. My parents died in a car accident when I was twenty years old. Liv, my sister, was eighteen. It was awful. But I understand what you're feeling," I said, putting my hand to my chest. "Right here. There's an unfillable hole."

He nodded quickly. "In the shape of my dad."

Ooof. That hit me right in the heart. I got all teary and he did too, but then he laughed. "Shit, I'm sorry. I didn't mean to burden you with all this. It's just this time of year . . . and then Ronny mentioned my dad, and . . ." He shook his head. "And it's Christmas."

"It's a hard time of year." I put my fork down, my plate empty.

"I haven't even put up a tree this year," he said with a shrug. "Just didn't feel right somehow."

"I had no Christmas decorations either. My apartment was all packed up, stuff was either sold or put into storage, and I stayed at a hotel for three days before I left." I sighed. "But I'm looking forward to Christmas with Liv."

He studied my eyes for a moment. "I bet you are."

I felt a bit scrutinised under his stare, those blue eyes were like sapphires, glinting in the soft light. "No boyfriend?" I asked. Because I had to ask. Lord, don't judge me. "I find it hard to believe the cutest guy in Hartbridge is single."

The corner of his lip curled upward. "How do you know I'm the cutest when you haven't met anyone else?"

"Well, because I have eyes. And honestly, the only guy who could beat your cuteness would be Chris Evans. Does Chris Evans live in Hartbridge?"

He was smiling now. "No, he does not."

"Then you win."

He chuckled. "No, there's no boyfriend. There hasn't been for a long time. Hartbridge isn't exactly gay central. What about you? Leave a trail of crying men at the airport?"

I snorted. "Uh, no. Some friends, sure. But no one was busting my door down begging me not to leave."

Ren took a deep breath and exhaled with a sigh. He opened his mouth to say something but a staticky buzz sounded and it startled me. "Oh, the radio," he said, standing up. Static crackled again as Ren opened the door and snatched up the receiver just as a guy finished saying something about taking a car back to town. "Thanks, Robert. Message received. Over."

"Should be able to take a look at it tomorrow. Over."

"Thanks for the call-out. We'll be in touch in the morning. Over and out." Ren hung the receiver in the cradle and gave me a smile. "Well, your car's taken care of. So that's one thing. We'll know tomorrow."

"Thank you," I said again. "I hate to think what I would have done if you hadn't come along."

He smiled, all lazy and warm. "I'm glad I found you."

Maybe there was a spark between us, or maybe I was so tired I was bordering on delirious. God, I wanted to stay up and find out if I was imagining it, but I could hardly keep my eyes open. "I think you were right about having a belly full of food. I wish I could stay up and talk more—I'd like to because you're kinda great—but I've been up for thirty-six hours. My brain's not working. As you could probably tell by the 'you're kinda great' comment."

He just kept right on smiling. "You should go to bed."

As much as I wished otherwise, I couldn't fight it. I nodded and went back to the table, taking my plate to the sink.

"Leave that," he said. "I'll take care of it."

I leaned against the counter, not minding one bit how close we were. "Ren?"

"Yeah?"

"I'm really glad you found me too."

CHAPTER FOUR

REN

HAMISH WAS JUST about dead on his feet. His blinks were getting longer and his head was nodding like it was too heavy to hold up. And heaven help me, I wanted him to stay up so we could chat all night long too, but there was no way.

I'm pretty sure he was asleep before he even got into bed, before his head was on the pillow.

I liked him. Talking to him was as easy as a summer breeze. I told him things I hadn't told anyone. For no other reason than it felt the right thing to do. Like my heart needed it, cathartic, exposed, and I thought I would feel ripped open when he went to bed and I was alone. But I didn't.

Sure, talking about my dad left me feeling a little raw. But I felt better after my conversation with Hamish. Like talking to him about my dad helped somehow. Normally, whenever someone mentioned my dad, it felt as though they'd taken a cheese grater to my heart. But it didn't this time.

He'd lost his parents too, so maybe it was because he understood. Maybe it was because he was a complete stranger and he hadn't grown up in this town and knew my dad all his life. He didn't look at me with pity.

He looked at me with those dark soulful eyes, his long dark lashes, and all I could see was understanding.

Weird, huh? That I'd known him for just a few hours and yet it felt like he knew me better than most people I'd known my whole life.

I was almost certain he was gay, or bi at least. I never liked to assume or judge people, and he could have been as straight as an arrow for all I knew. But his eyes would fall to my lips too often for it to be nothing. Straight men didn't do that. They just didn't. Well, not any I've ever met. Not to mention Hamish's voice was melodic and he talked while using his hands with a flourish, and I was pretty sure he put on some kind of lip balm after his shower . . .

But I had to know for sure.

And, if I was being truthful, I wanted to be honest with him. I wanted him to know about that part of me.

I couldn't tell you why I wanted him to know, apart from the honesty thing. But why divulge this part of myself to him? A passing stranger who would, in all likelihood, be gone the next day. And it was a secret some guys didn't take too kindly to hearing. I wasn't naïve enough to know that it could have ended badly. He could have ranted some homophobic tirade at me and walked out into the snowstorm.

But my heart told me to tell him. I almost couldn't get the words out, but thankfully it wasn't like I had to spell it out for him. He got it, because he understood.

Seriously, it was just good to speak to someone who was gay. I wasn't kidding when I said it had been a long time for me. But talking about things that I couldn't talk about with anyone, like boyfriends or dating, felt so damn good. Things that didn't need explaining, things he understood.

That felt like a tiny piece of home.

It made me realise I did miss being part of the LGBTQ community. As much as I loved my life here in Hartbridge, there would always be that part of me here that was missing.

And now that I knew it was missing, I had to wonder what that meant for me. After Hamish was long gone, where did that leave me?

Maybe I could start making an effort. Maybe I could find some groups that met in a nearby town. Bars and clubs weren't my style, but maybe there was a monthly meet-up or book club or something.

Maybe.

Maybe it was all too hard.

Maybe if Hamish was staying with his sister we could catch up on a weekend every now and then and just talk. It was only a ninety-minute drive.

God, was I that desperate?

The CB radio startled me from scrubbing the sink and I ducked out into the mudroom to grab it. It was Ronny letting me know he'd got hold of the local guys in Mossley and they sent out word to Hamish's sister. She was very relieved and burst into tears at the news, apparently, but she knew he was alive and he was safe.

I thanked Ronny and turned the radio off, amazed at how stupidly relieved I was for Hamish. He would be so happy to know his sister had been told. I wondered if he was still awake and poked my head into his room. It was dark, obviously, but I could see he was sound asleep. All tucked in warm, breathing deep, and I didn't have the heart to wake him, so I found my notepad and wrote him a quick note. Given he was asleep before six o'clock, if he woke up at three in the morning, he'd want to know his sister had been told.

Hamish, your sister knows you're here and that you're okay. Thought you'd want to know.

I tiptoed into his room and slipped the note onto his phone on the bedside table. He'd see it first thing.

After that, I parked up on the couch with Chutney and settled in for a movie. It had been my sole intention for my three days off—to watch movies and read books—but I found my mind wondering. Not even *The First Wives Club* could hold my attention.

All I could think about was dark brown eyes, the longest eyelashes I'd ever seen, and a cute-as-hell Australian accent.

So I apologised to Diane Keaton and watched Hugh Jackman in the movie *Australia* instead.

I WOKE UP, and for a few seconds I'd forgotten there was someone else in the house. I couldn't hear anyone up, and Chutney was still asleep on my bed, so I assumed Hamish hadn't surfaced yet.

I'd heard jetlag could really mess some people up, and without knowing if he'd be awake any time soon, I figured I'd just get on with my day. I gave Chutney some breakfast, stoked the fire, and filled the coffee machine before I grabbed a quick shower. I was hoping the noise would wake him, as selfish as that was.

Then I set about making some breakfast. Coffee, toast, eggs, and bacon, and sure enough, the smell brought him out of his room. Or maybe it was me accidently being the noisiest cook on the planet.

He was all sleep rumpled, one eye half-closed, his dark hair was flat on one side, sticking up on the other, and he might have been the cutest thing I'd ever seen.

"Oh, morning," I said brightly. "Hope I didn't wake you." Which was a bald-face lie but he didn't know that.

He squinted one eye shut. "Smells good."

"Take a seat, I'll serve it up."

"Gimme one sec, please," he mumbled, then disappeared into the bathroom. A few minutes later, he came out a little more awake. He'd clearly splashed water on his face and tried to do something with his hair. "Sorry. Not really a morning person."

"Do you drink coffee?" I asked.

He nodded. "Inhale it, bathe in it, drink it."

I chuckled and handed him a cup. "Sleep okay?"

He sipped his coffee and nodded. "Like the dead." He took another sip. "This is great, thank you." Then he held up his phone and the note. "Still no phone service, but I got the note. Thank you. I really appreciate you doing that for me."

"I thought you'd want to know as soon as you woke up. I was going to wake you last night but you were so tired."

He smiled. "I woke up around half three. I checked the time and found the note then. I forgot where I was, so at first I thought it was some kind of kidnapping note or a ransom thing, but then I remembered."

I laughed and gestured to the table. "You hungry? I wasn't sure when you'd wake up, but I made enough for two."

"I am, though I don't know how. All you've done is feed me."

I pulled his chair out and he ducked his head and

smiled as he sat. "So, you said you woke up at half three. Is that a code or a euphemism for something?"

He put his coffee down as he laughed. "Ah no, sorry. Half three is three thirty. I don't really know what's Australian or not so I don't know what not to say."

"Don't change anything," I said, sitting opposite him. "I like it."

His cheeks tinted pink and he chewed on his bottom lip, focusing instead on the food on the table. "This looks great."

"Help yourself to whatever you want." I dished myself up some eggs and bacon and bit into a slice of toast. "I don't normally cook breakfast. Except for holidays and maybe a long weekend."

Hamish plated up some bacon and eggs. "How many days will you have off over Christmas?"

"Just three. Well, kinda four if you include the half-day yesterday. I'll go back the day after Christmas."

"The store must keep you busy?"

"Yep, but that's a good thing. Means business is good, right?"

"Yeah, of course. Is it just you that works there?"

"Mrs Barton does my accounts, just a few hours three days a week, and helps out in the store sometimes. She's worked there since I can remember." I ate some eggs and swallowed. "She's always been a bit of a mother figure to me, and she was a godsend when my dad died. Sweet as candy, she is."

"Nice," he replied, sipping his coffee with a smile. "I have two weeks off, then it's back to work for me. My company is almost all online now, so I can work from anywhere. We have underwriters and whatnot based here in the States, so when I spoke to my boss about leaving, she gave me the option of transferring out. It was a no brainer, really."

"That worked out really well."

"Yeah, and I figured if I got here and found something better, I'd just quit. But I'll need something till I get on my feet, ya know?"

I nodded. "Definitely. I can't imagine just packing up and moving to a different country. On the other side of the planet."

He grinned. "I wasn't sure I could do it. Almost didn't survive day one, so I probably shouldn't jinx myself."

I chuckled. "Well, let's hope day two is a better one. Though the sun's out so I'm thinking that's a start. Phone lines should be up soon too, I'd guess. They're never usually down for this long."

He turned to look out the window, like he'd forgotten all about the snow outside. His eyes went wide and his whole face lit up. He stood and went for a closer look, like . . . well, like he'd never seen anything like it. "I've never seen anything like it," he whispered.

I chuckled and joined him by the window. Outside was a few feet of white, powdery snow. The trees were frosted with it. The early morning sunshine glowed like a dream. "Wanna go out in it?"

He shot me a look. "Can I?"

I laughed. "Of course you can."

"Oh, I'm not dressed or showered or anything." Then his gaze met mine, excited and a little scared. "Oh my God, what do I wear?"

His excitement was contagious. "Save your shower for when you come back inside and need to thaw out. Do you have boots?"

"I have a pair of Gucci boots I bought on sale."

I snorted. "Uh, no. I can loan you some. What size are you?"

"A ten."

"Well, they'll be big on you but you can wear them."

"Oh, what size . . ." His gaze went to my socked feet. "Oh my, what big . . . feet you have."

I chuckled, and a warmth spread in my belly. He was so close I could feel the heat of his body, and I wanted to touch him, his arm, his back, his cheek, those pink lips . . .

But it was hardly appropriate. He was stuck here, for lack of a better word, without a car or phone. To pressure him into anything unwanted would be horrible and he might feel obligated or threatened, and that was akin to a cold shower. I took a step back. "I'll go find those boots," I said. "As for pants, do you have thermals?"

"Uh, no."

"Long johns?"

"Long what?"

I tried not to smile. "You wear them under your jeans or pants."

"Like leggings or tights?" He sniffed. "I may be a little fem, I'll admit, but the last time I wore tights was to a fancy-dress ball. I went with Emma, a friend from the office. We went as Belle and the Beast. And I have to say, I rocked that yellow ball gown, but the heels killed me."

I laughed again. My God, he was funny. "Okay, let me see what I can find."

When I came back out with some warmer clothes for him, he'd cleaned up most of the breakfast mess I'd made. He was standing at the sink, wearing his expensive loungewear, with a tea towel thrown over his shoulder, looking cute as hell wiping everything down.

And it hit me, with a pang of want and reality, that I

could have this. Not Hamish. But I could have someone to share my life with, who could wear his PJs around the house, who would smile when he saw me like Hamish did.

I could have this.

And as much as I liked having Hamish here, the worst part of seeing him being all cute in his PJs was that now I knew I wanted it.

I'd convinced myself all this time that I didn't need it. That I was content with my store, my home, my life in Hartbridge, just as it was. I didn't think I could want anything more. I certainly didn't think it was possible.

And now I wasn't sure. Maybe it was.

"Everything okay?" Hamish asked.

I'd been standing there, holding the clothes and staring at him like an idiot.

"I wasn't sure where anything went," he added uncertainly, gesturing to the things he'd dried but left on the counter.

"Oh, that's perfect. You didn't have to clean anything up; you're a guest here."

"Hardly. It's the least I could do after all you've done for me."

"It's no trouble at all," I said, quieter than I'd meant to. "Uh, here are some thermals. They're clean, I promise. I haven't worn them for years."

He took them and smiled kindly, just standing there right in front of me. "Thank you."

I swallowed hard and nodded, and only when his bedroom door snicked close did I exhale. How was it possible to lose my mind after just a few hours with him? It hadn't even been a day!

Chutney yipped at my feet, which cleared my head a little, so I gave her the bacon that was left and grabbed her coat. I was putting her shoes on when Hamish came out. "Your dog has a coat. And shoes?" he asked. "That's the cutest thing I've ever seen!"

I grinned up at him. "I have to keep my baby warm. Last winter when she was just a puppy, she ran through the snow because she loves it, but she almost froze to death." I shrugged. "And she has to go potty."

"Fair enough. When a girl's gotta go, she has to go." He was wearing some navy pants and a sweater but he was holding a coat. A very pink coat, but at least it looked warm. "These pants will have to do. Believe me when I say, nothing else was fitting into my skinny jeans. I really need to go shopping for snow clothes." He stuck his foot out. "But the socks you loaned me are the best things ever. You'll need to tell me where you got them from."

"Mrs Barton knits them."

"Oh my God, for real?"

I nodded. "Sure does."

"I didn't know knitting socks was a thing." He sat on the couch and pulled on the boots I'd got for him. They were miles too big, but at least they'd keep him warm. He did up the laces and stood up, waved his hand, and did a perfect David Rose impression. "'And these mountaineering shoes that my boyfriend is wearing, looking like Oprah going on a Thanksgiving Day hike.'"

I laughed. "Love that show."

"Same." He lifted one boot up. "There is a very good chance that I will trip and injure myself wearing these."

"You'll be fine," I said, pulling my boots on. "Got a hat?"

He pulled out a knitted cap that matched his pink coat and grinned. "I have a beanie. It matches."

I laughed. "I can see that."

He made a face, unsure and maybe a little embarrassed. "Is it too much pink?"

"Can there ever be too much pink?"

His smile was magnificent and he sighed happily. "Absolutely not. 'Whoever said orange was the new pink was seriously disturbed.'"

"Oh my God," I whispered, grinning as my heart did a little dance with the butterflies in my belly. "You just quoted *Legally Blonde*."

He beamed. "I told you I loved it."

I don't know why it affected me so much, but it made me happy and a little bit sad. "I don't get to really talk about stuff I like," I admitted. "Not with my friends here. I mean, I could, I guess. I just don't."

Hamish frowned. "Would they shun you? Or laugh at you for that kind of thing?"

"No, I don't think so." I shrugged. "I just don't share that part of myself." I sighed and shook my head, feeling a bit foolish for admitting this to him. "Come on, Miss Chutney will pee on the floor if we don't hurry."

"Oh!" He looked at Chutney, panicked. "Quick!" He turned the door handle, opened the door, and stopped. He stood, stock still, horrified. "Nope." Then he closed the door.

I laughed and handed him a pair of gloves. "Come on, it's not that bad."

Chutney followed me out onto the porch and did a little dance when I picked up the shovel. I looked back at Hamish, who was staring, somewhat horrified. "What are you doing with that?"

"I gotta shovel. It's what happens when it snows." And truth be told, it hadn't even snowed too much. Maybe a few feet. I scraped off the steps and began making a path for

Chutney. "Come on, shut the door. You're letting all the heat out."

That made him move, at least. He stepped out and pulled the door shut behind him. "Oh, sorry."

I tried not to watch him too much. I didn't want to come off as creepy, but it was cute as hell watching him experience snow for the first time. He crouched down at the steps, took his glove off, and poked his pointer finger into the bed of white powder. He grinned and did it again, but then quickly put his glove back on. He scooped up a handful, and still on his haunches, he inspected it, poked at it, then looked at me and grinned. "Can I taste it?"

I chuckled. "Sure you can."

He lifted the scoop to his face, stuck out his tongue, and tentatively tasted the snow. There was a brief moment of confusion on his face, then he brought it to his lips and tasted it properly. He dumped the scoop onto the snow and brushed his hands as he stood up. "It tastes like when I was about seven and I stuck my tongue to the inside of the freezer."

I snorted. "You didn't do that, did you?"

He made a face. "No."

He totally did. Laughing, I shovelled for a bit, making a bit of a path along the side of the house toward the garage, and when I turned around, he was staring at me. "You all right there?"

"Only down one side."

"What?"

"I'm left down the other." He smiled. "Actually, I was just enjoying the view."

The view. Right. He was staring at my ass. I grinned at him and held the shovel out. "Want a go?"

"Sure," he said, carefully walking down the wet steps

and he took the shovel and actually gave it a real go. He was pretty good at it for a first time, and I liked that he didn't even blink at the mention of hard work.

We got a path cleared and Chutney did her thing, and I cleared some more toward the garage. But then Hamish lifted his foot and stomped down into the bank of snow. And he froze and shrieked. "Oh my God!"

I rushed to him, thinking something was wrong. "What is it?"

"It sounds like how cotton wool balls feel."

Uh . . .

It sounds like how cotton wool balls feel. I had to repeat that in my head to see if I could make sense of it. I barked out a laugh. "Um, what?"

He still had his foot stuck in the snow. "You know that awful cotton wool ball feeling?" He held his arm out for me to help him. "It's squelchy but dry and it's like fingers down a chalkboard. Oh my God, it's so bad."

Chuckling, I put my arm around his shoulder and kind of lifted him out, putting him down on his two feet on the path. "Better?"

He looked up at me, so close our fronts were almost touching. He nodded slowly. "Much."

My God, his eyes were so brown, they were like burned honey or malt whiskey . . . I could just melt into them.

"You warm enough?" I asked, ignoring how low and gruff my voice was.

He nodded again. "Yeah."

Then Chutney had to take a running dive into the snow, yapping and having the best time of her life. Which was a great distraction and Hamish laughed and followed her along the path, which was also great because I was about two seconds away from something stupid like kissing him.

Boy, I needed to get a grip.

Hamish was still laughing at Chutney, who was now jumping through three feet of snow, and he looked at me with the happiest, sweetest smile.

It made my heart ache.

But then something buzzed and Hamish froze. It buzzed again and he threw his hands up and began patting himself down. "My phone! We must have mobile reception."

He found his phone in his inside coat pocket and pulled it. If I thought he was happy before . . .

"Holy shit. So many messages, so many missed calls. Three bars," he said, holding it up to show me. Then it rang again in his hand and I thought for a second he was too excited to answer it, but he shrieked first, then answered it. "Olivia!" He nodded and I could hear her excited shrieking through the phone. Then, still with his phone to his ear, Hamish put his other hand over his eyes and burst into tears.

Oh, man.

I didn't know if she'd just dropped a horrible bombshell or if he was just overwhelmed. I was thinking it was the latter. I put the shovel down, took his hand, and led him up the porch steps, helped him out of his boots and inside the house. I sat him on the couch and pulled off his beanie. "I'll just be outside," I whispered.

He nodded and gave me a sad smile. He mouthed the words thank you to me, then spoke into the phone. "Of course I'm crying. Bloody hell, Olivia, do you not know me at all?"

I left him to it, happier now I was sure he was just overwhelmed and hadn't received bad news. He clearly missed her like crazy, and he'd come so far to see her and metaphorically tripped over the last hurdle before the finish line.

I needed to clear more of a path to my garage. Then we could drive in town and see if his car was fixable or if the rental place could organise another one. The poor guy needed to see his sister, and I needed to help him. Enough of the selfish reasons I wanted him to stay, I needed to do everything I could to help him leave.

Leaning the shovel resting against the house, I picked up Chutney and trudged through the snow toward the garage.

CHAPTER FIVE

HAMISH

"WHAT DO you mean he's gorgeous?"

"I mean he's fucking gorgeous," I repeated. After I'd stopped blubbering, I'd explained my disaster of a day yesterday to my sister and, of course, that led to the part where I was rescued by the handsome stranger. "He's gay, he's single, he owns his own business. He lives in a cute-as-hell cabin-type house. He's sweet and funny, and Liv, I don't think you understand. He even named his dog Chutney from *Legally Blonde*. And he has little shoes for her so she can walk in the snow."

"Oh hell, Hamish," she replied. "He's perfect for you."

"Right now," I added, peeking through the curtains to the front of the house. "He's riding on some lawnmower with a scoopy thing at the front, plowing snow off his driveway. And Chutney is on his knee." I shook my head, flummoxed by his perfectness. "But I gotta say, Liv. What is up with the snow?"

She laughed. "Beautiful, isn't it?"

I sighed, watching Ren as he did another lap. "It sure is."

"Are you even going to want to leave him to come see me?"

I snorted. "Yeah, of course." But the idea of never seeing Ren again didn't sit well with me. "I mean, I can do the casual 'I was just in town so I thought I'd call in' thing, can't I? Not that I'd know what to look for in a hardware store."

Liv laughed. "You'd be looking for the owner by the sounds of it."

"Which is ridiculous. I don't know if he even likes me like that or if he's even interested . . . God. But he sure is cute." I sighed again. "It's like I landed in a Hallmark movie."

"Oooh, those Christmas movies are like sugar. You know you shouldn't love them but you totally do. All the smiling people and houses with more Christmas decorations than a department store."

That was so true. Ren had said he hadn't bothered with a Christmas tree, but I only kind of noticed there were no decorations up anywhere. No tree, no wreath on the door, no garland thingies hanging around the fireplace. Not one thing.

How odd. Tomorrow was Christmas Eve . . .

Maybe he didn't celebrate it like that? Maybe his tradition was to decorate on Christmas Eve? Maybe they only decorated a tree and he wasn't doing that this year.

Maybe it was none of my business.

But it hurt my heart to think he'd be sad at Christmas.

Ren drove his little snowplow back to the garage and I heard the motor cut off. "Hey, Liv. I gotta go. I'll be in touch when I know about the car."

"We can always come get you," she offered again. "Josh finishes work at one."

"If it comes to that, I'll let you know. Hopefully it'll all be fine, the car is fixed, and I'll see you before lunch."

She made an *eeeeeeeek* sound. "I hope so too. I can't wait."

"Me too."

"And drive carefully this time! No running off the road. I almost had a heart attack when the police showed up here to tell me you were okay. I thought you'd been hurt or were dead or something."

"I'm sorry. I didn't know how else to contact you. Ren suggested it."

"Well, tell him I said thanks. And that's not sarcasm. Once I got over the heart attack, I was so relieved that you were okay. And here! God, I can't believe you're actually here!"

I smiled. "Same. I'll see you soon."

After I'd disconnected the call, I pulled my beanie back on and went out onto the porch. Ren was walking up with a bouncy Chutney behind him. "Everything okay?" he asked.

"Oh yeah, sorry about before," I replied. "I don't know why I cried. I mean, I cry all the time—sad movies, happy movies, the news, animal rescue videos on YouTube. I was just so happy to hear her voice."

He got to the stairs and kicked the snow off the boots. "I cleared the driveway. We can go see about your car. We'll get you back on the road. If not, I can drive you there. It's really not that far."

I smiled at him. "Thank you. For everything."

He pulled his beanie off. "Let me just grab my keys and wallet."

"Oh, we're leaving now?" But that was so soon!

"Well, I thought you'd want to . . ." He made a face, but quickly dried Chutney off with an old towel.

God, I think he wants me to go.

"Uh, sure. Of course. Just let me grab my bags." I dashed to my room and shoved everything back into my suitcase. "Uh, did you want me to strip the bed? I can change the sheets before I go," I called out.

He was standing at the door, leaning against the frame, and smiling at me trying to zip up the suitcase. "It's fine. I'll take care of that."

I took my phone charger and plug converter from the wall and shoved it into my backpack. "I think that's everything."

Ren swallowed and nodded, finding something in the hall fascinating. "Uh, okay then."

"Oh, the thermal pants and the socks," I remembered, looking down at my feet. "I can get changed."

He put his hand up and the corner of his mouth lifted. "You can keep them. And the boots. You're gonna need them, most likely. Until you can get your own."

"Right," I mumbled, feeling a bit foolish. "When Liv said it was cold and I should pack accordingly, I grossly underestimated her definition of cold."

That earned me a smile. He stepped into the room and took the biggest suitcase.

"That's the one with the broken wheel," I said.

"I could probably fix it," he offered. "It's just a caster wheel. We have them at the store."

"I wouldn't worry too much. As soon as I find a place of my own, I won't be needing it anymore." I stood there, unsure of what to say or do. I wanted to go see my sister, I really did. But I wasn't too keen on saying goodbye to Ren just yet. And from the way he just stood there too, maybe he didn't want me to go just yet either?

I cleared my throat. "So, I . . ."

"Yes," he said, lifting the bag. "We should leave."

He was gone before I could say anything, because leaving was not what I was going to suggest . . . but instead, I followed him out without a word.

He grabbed his keys and wallet, did something to the fire to keep it going, then locked the door behind us. Chutney was excited because she obviously liked going on adventures, and I managed walking to the garage without dying. I did slip and slide a little but the boots Ren gave me were a lifesaver.

"You okay?" he asked, lifting my bags into the back of his ute. Sorry, truck. Ugh.

"Yeah, definitely. Was just thinking of upgrading my gay status from queen to butch with these boots. They're great."

Ren barked out a laugh. "Gay status is a thing? I must have missed the memo." He picked Chutney up and opened the passenger door, placing her inside.

"Oh, the gay memo. Yeah, it's like the letter from Hogwarts. And Hagrid appears and says 'yer a gay now, Harry.'"

He laughed again. "He must have got lost."

"Maybe he was an Aussie Hagrid who couldn't drive in the snow."

He chuckled. "Maybe." Then he made a thoughtful face. "What status would I have got? I'm not exactly queen-ish or butch, I don't think."

"You're the perfect status. Not many can claim that. It's like the Sorting Hat put you in Gryffindor, but for gays."

That made him laugh. "Perfect?"

"Yep. And the Sorting Hat is never wrong."

He was still holding the door open and I realised, a little

belatedly, that he was holding it for me. "See? Perfect," I said as I climbed in.

He closed the door and smiled as he walked around the front of the truck. When he got in, Chutney was on my lap, doing her little happy dance. He rolled his eyes and shook his head, laughing as he started his truck. "She likes you."

"I'm a likeable guy."

The truck chugged out of the garage and Ren shot me a quick look. "You are, Hamish. I'm sorry you got stuck and missed out on seeing your sister yesterday. But I'm glad I met you." He shifted in his seat, uncomfortable. "I don't get to talk to . . . to other guys very often. It's been . . . nice."

"It has been nice," I agreed. "Getting rescued by a guy who was not a grizzly bear or a serial killer. Who fed me, organised to get my car towed and for the cops to let my sister know I wasn't dead." I gave Chutney a pat. "But seriously, it was better than nice. It was lovely. I had a lovely time, thank you."

He turned the truck out of his drive and onto the road. Everything was white, though the road had been plowed at some point. The sides of the road were banks of snow, and I'd never seen anything like it.

"See there," he said, pointing to the side of the road. "That's where I found you."

It was a lot of snow. Though I could see now if the snow hadn't stopped me, the trees sure would have. It looked a lot scarier now I could actually see it. "Oh, wow."

Chutney was still on my lap and we looked out the window at the passing scenery. It was mostly just snow and trees. A few driveways, but the road was winding and I must have been crazy to think I could drive in this.

After a few beats of silence, he said. "You're right. What

you said before. It was better than nice. I enjoyed having the company."

"I enjoyed it too," I admitted. "And sure, I'd have loved to have seen my sister yesterday, but I'm not at all disappointed I got to spend time with you." I gave Chutney another pat, given she'd gone from standing on my lap and looking out the window to now sitting on my lap enjoying my attention. Then, while I still had the courage, I added, "And you know, if it's just ninety minutes away, I can come visit you in your shop. I can bring morning tea or something. Or we can do dinner and we talk about all the gayness you want. Make a day of it."

Ren's smile became a grin. "I'd like that."

I sighed, happy and relieved that even though we were saying goodbye today, it wasn't goodbye forever, and I turned my attention to the scenery. I could see mountains now, more trees and more snow. Everything was white and so beautiful. But then we came up over a rise and on the other side was a valley, a river, and a small town. Not just any old small town, but possibly the prettiest small town I'd ever seen. The main street was lined with quaint stores with awnings and vintage signs, painted windows, and Christmas decorations hanging from streetlamps. Snow made everything glisten like a dream.

"Are you kidding me?" I asked, wide-eyed and smiling.

"What?" Ren asked.

"I *did* land in a Hallmark movie! This is a freaking Hallmark Christmas movie set! Actually, the last twenty-four hours have been straight out of a Hallmark movie, I'm sure of it. I think I hit my head when my car ran off the road." I put my hand to my forehead. "I'm dreaming, aren't I?"

Ren snorted. "Uh, no?"

"Pretty sure that's what all gorgeous Hallmark movie guys say."

"Gorgeous?"

"Utterly."

He pulled the truck over to the kerb and shut the engine off. He turned in his seat to look at me. "You didn't hit your head yesterday. You're not dreaming. This is Hartbridge. It's not a Hallmark movie set." He shrugged, amused. "Though it could be, I guess."

"It should be."

His gaze met mine, and for a long moment, neither of us moved. Then his eyes dropped to my lips, and for a heart-stopping second, I thought he might ask to kiss me. But then he blinked and startled, shifting his focus out his window. "Right, well, here it is. McGee's Mechanics," he said, opening his door.

I took a hold of Chutney and carried her out of the ute . . . err, truck, and walked around to the footpath . . . err, sidewalk. God.

The mechanic's shop was a white brick building with big roller doors at the front which were pulled down. "Are they open?"

Ren checked his watch. "Should be. It's after nine. He keeps the garage doors down if he's quiet and if it's cold out." He went to what I assumed was an office door, opened it, and called out, "Robert, you in?"

"Is that you, Ren?" came the reply.

"Sure is."

"Yeah, come through. Thought I heard your truck."

We walked through a small reception office area into the shop. It smelled of oil and grease, there was an old car up on a hoist, and my rental car on the ground with its bonnet up . . . err, its hood up. Robert was an older gent in blue overalls, with short grey hair and a broad smile.

Ren made quick introductions and got straight to business. "So, is there any damage?"

"It's good news," he said. "Just a loose connection and some water or moisture in the power control module. Happens sometimes when snow gets where it shouldn't."

"Can you fix it?" I asked. "I have to drive to my sister's in Mossley."

"Well, I can fix it, no problem. As soon as I hear from the rental company, anyway," he replied in that old-man drawl. "But you won't be driving to Mossley today. Beartrap Road is closed in both directions. They're working to get it cleared, but it won't be for a good few hours yet, if today at all. Tomorrow's your day, if you got somewhere you can stay tonight. I think the motel is full, but you could try calling them."

My heart sank. "Oh."

They went on talking about the road and snow and powerlines and how the rental company had been notified and the paperwork had been sent, but I couldn't pay any attention.

I wasn't going to see Liv today . . .

"You okay?" Ren asked me quietly.

I tried to smile. It wasn't anyone's fault; well, not if you didn't include my disaster self's fault for driving into a snowbank yesterday. It was just bad luck. "Yeah. It's just that tomorrow's Christmas Eve, and I was supposed to be there yesterday and I haven't seen Liv in four years and she's so close but it may as well be a million miles."

Ren put his hand on my shoulder. "We'll get you there tomorrow. I promise. One way or another."

Just then, my phone rang, and I tried to fish it out of my

pocket while still holding Chutney. Ren took her; I got my phone out and saw Liv's name on-screen. "I better take this," I said. "Sorry."

I ducked back out into the reception and out onto the footpath. "Hey," I answered.

"Hamish, Josh just called me from work to tell me the road's closed!"

"I know. I just found out. The mechanic said he could fix my car but the road is blocked or something. I dunno. Liv, I won't get to see you today," I said, trying not to cry. My disappointment was palpable, visceral, aching. "It sucks that I'm so close and I can't get there. Isn't there another road?"

"Not from where you are. Unless you went south about a hundred miles and then came across and back up. But that would take you all day with the snow and all, and it's all mountain road, Hamish. I don't know if those roads are any better."

I sighed and kicked my toe into a clump of snow near the gutter. "It's so unfair. It better be cleared by tomorrow. Tomorrow's Christmas Eve, Liv."

"I know," she whispered. "But you're here, that's the main thing."

I frowned, feeling miserable for myself. I didn't even know where I could stay the night . . . I needed to get stuff sorted. Surely there was more than one motel in town. *Surely.* "Well, I better go back in and sort out this car. He said something about paperwork. Can we FaceTime later? I miss your face."

"Yes!" she laughed. "I miss your face too."

"Bye, Liv."

"I will see you soon!"

I nodded, though I didn't feel as optimistic as her. I

clicked off the call and sighed, looking up the pretty street. It was so picturesque it hardly seemed real. There were some people walking, another truck driving down the road, and Christmas decorations just about everywhere. For a town so pretty, there had to be holiday accommodation. I began to thumb in a search for an Airbnb when Ren's voice startled me. "Everything okay?"

He looked so concerned, I felt bad for making him worry. Chutney was all smiles as she walked and sniffed, and so help me, the two of them were just the cutest. "Yeah, I just … Liv was ringing to tell me about the road being closed. Which sucks."

"Yeah, Beartrap Road is the only road in from here. If it's closed, there's no way in."

"What the hell kind of name is Beartrap Road?" I asked, horrified. "And what should I be more terrified of? The bear or the trap? And pray tell, who the hell is trapping bears? Just leave the fluffy killing machines alone." He laughed, and I sighed. "Sorry. I tend to ramble when I'm stressed."

His smile twisted into a bit of a pout. "I'm sorry you can't see your sister today."

"Me too."

"Robert said he'll call when he hears from the car rental place and what they want to do. They should send a replacement vehicle, but honestly, it'd be quicker for this one to be fixed."

"Is his name really Robert McGee?" I asked quietly. "As in Bobby McGee?"

Ren chuckled. "That's why he goes by Robert."

I nodded and shrugged when I remembered my phone in my hand. "I was just searching for an Airbnb or some holiday rental. Do you know of anyone who rents out a room?"

He frowned and looked up the street, then scratched the back of his neck. "Well, yeah."

"If you say Norman Bates, I'll take my chances on Beartrap Road."

He chuckled and met my eyes. "Me."

"You rent out rooms?"

"No, I meant you could just stay with me. Another night, if you like."

"Are you sure? I've really been more than an inconvenience, and you've gone above and beyond. I can't ask any more of you."

He put his hand on my arm. "Hamish, it's no problem. I've really enjoyed having you stay. I was fully prepared to be alone and do nothing but watch movies, but having someone to talk to has been . . . well, it's been great." He blushed and looked decidedly uncomfortable, and I missed his touch when he let his hand fall away.

"Are you sure?" I asked. "I'd hate to be a bother. I could make you dinner as a thank you. But a word of warning, I'm not a very good cook, and as long as you have a fire extinguisher handy, we'll be fine. And maybe an evacuation plan, just in case."

He chuckled again. "Or I could cook you dinner. I rather like my house not on fire, thanks."

I sighed, long and loud. "I really am very grateful. Thank you. For everything."

Ren met my gaze, his blue eyes glittering like the snow. "You're welcome. And like I said before, I've enjoyed having you stay."

"We can talk about all the gayness things you don't get to talk about with the good folks here. Whatever you want," I said adamantly. "*Project Runway, Ru Paul's Drag Race,*

Schitt's Creek, Xena, He-Man and the Masters of the Universe."

"*He-Man?*"

I nodded, very matter of fact. "Long boots, a harness, and a codpiece."

Ren burst out laughing. "Don't forget his broadsword."

I gasped. "You get it."

Smiling, with his hand on my lower back, he nodded to his truck. "Come on, let's go home."

CHAPTER SIX

REN

HOME. I just said "let's go home" like it was *our* home, like he belonged there, and I couldn't even be mad about it. It just rolled off my tongue and it felt nice.

Okay, so *nice* was an understatement, but to call it anything else would have called for closer examination and I wasn't quite ready to go there yet.

Words like wonderful and exciting, and the scariest one of all . . . it felt *right*.

I wasn't ready to examine that yet. To pull that apart would mean admitting the fact that I did want someone in my life and that a life of loneliness was not what I wanted like I'd convinced myself I did.

Having Hamish stay, even for just one or two days, was enough for me to realise that maybe I didn't have to settle for a half-life. Maybe I didn't have to settle for loneliness as a trade-off for wanting to live in Hartbridge.

"Should we call into a supermarket? If you're going to cook dinner, the least I could do is buy the stuff for it," Hamish asked as we walked over to my truck. Then he stopped. "Oh, does Hartbridge have a supermarket?"

I laughed. "I'll have you know, we have the wonderful Hartbridge Home Market. Sells everything we could ever need." I opened my door. "Between you and me, it's about the size of a 7-Eleven and I have to order a lot of stuff online."

Hamish laughed and pulled his door open. I put Chutney in the truck, and as soon as Hamish climbed in, she was on his lap, the both of them grinning out the window. "We don't need any food for dinner. My fridge is stocked full. Unless you needed anything?"

"No, I don't need anything," he said happily. "Well, apart from thermal underwear and decent gloves, and boots more appropriate for snow, but I highly doubt your Home Market sells those."

"Ah, we have men's apparel at Harold's,' I explained. "But he's closed for the holidays. Same for the fishing and rec store down by the river. Everyone closes for the three days, sorry."

"I don't mind," he replied, seemingly happy enough. I was glad he wasn't too upset over not being able to see his sister. I could understand his disappointment and I did feel sorry for him, but there was a tiny piece of me that was self-ishly not disappointed he was staying another night.

Main Street was as good as empty, so I pulled the truck up alongside the curb and pointed to my windowfront. "There's my second home." The sign clearly read Hart-bridge Hardware, so I didn't need to explain. The building itself was mostly brown brick and siding with an awning out the front, and while the sign looked vintage, it was new and just made to look that way.

Hamish looked at it for a long time, and when he turned to me, his eyes were warm and kind. "It's gorgeous."

I don't know why that made me so happy. He could have been indifferent or not cared at all, or worse, thought it was lame. But he genuinely liked it. "The service counter is original," I explained. "My grandpa made it and it's now so worn and smooth by seventy years of use. When I touch it, it reminds me that my grandpa and my dad's hands did that; made it smooth and slightly worn where they stood with their hands on it. I can feel their history, my history." I scoffed at how stupid that probably sounded to him. "Sorry, that must sound weird to you."

"Are you kidding me?" His voice was quiet, and when I met his gaze, I could see his eyes were glassy. "That's the single most beautiful thing I've ever heard. It's proof, ya know? It's a testament to them and now to you for carrying on their name, their hard work."

I nodded, getting a little teary myself. "There's a mark on the wall behind the office desk from my dad's chair. He was always going to putty it up and paint over it . . ." I took a shaky breath. "Now that he's gone, I can't bring myself to fix it."

"Don't ever fix it," he replied gently. "Leave it forever, and every time you see it, I hope it makes you smile."

I nodded, blinking back tears. I wasn't expecting to get so emotional. I guess talking about my grandpa and dad and knowing that when Hamish left tomorrow, I really would be spending Christmas alone, just kinda hit me harder than I realised.

Of course, Chutney chose that exact moment to start barking, probably wondering why we weren't going inside the shop. I wasn't sure if I was up for seeing that service counter right now. "Yeah, okay, okay," I said, putting my truck into gear. "We're going. Keep your socks on."

"She has got her socks on, Daddy," Hamish said, smiling all perfect and lifting her little foot to show me. Then, as we made our way home, he proceeded to point things out to her out his window, to which she listened intently, and I didn't know who out of the three of us was smiling the most.

AFTER HELPING Hamish take his suitcases back to his room, I went to the fridge to ask him what he'd prefer for dinner. "I have beef brisket, pork, and some chicken. I also have a stack of fresh veggies and I can make a pretty mean vegetable pasta. Or I can cook us a roast dinner. I can make either."

Hamish leaned against the kitchen cupboards, facing me. "Pasta sounds amazing."

"Too easy. And that won't take long at all."

"Can I make you a coffee?" he asked. "If you don't mind me using your kitchen. I feel like I should be doing something to help."

"Um, sure. Coffee sounds great."

He didn't know how to use my coffee machine or where anything was kept, and I had to help him with all of it, but it was fun to be moving around my kitchen with him. In no time at all, we had our fresh brews and he wanted to go back out into the snow.

"I just can't believe I'm here," he said, slowly walking down the front steps and along the path in the snow. "Finally. I mean, here in America. It seems like I started planning this forever ago."

"I've said it before, but I can't imagine just moving to the other side of the planet."

"It's not as scary as it sounds. More of a logistical pain in my arse."

"Where were you thinking of settling in?" I asked, trying to sound casual. I sipped my coffee and looked toward the tree line. "Somewhere close to your sister?"

"I was thinking, yes. I don't know how close though. Same town, maybe. I've never seen Mossley before. Is it as pretty as Hartbridge?" I shrugged because I was biased, and he laughed. "Nowhere is as pretty as Hartbridge, right?"

I chuckled at that. "I am unashamedly biased. But yes, Mossley is okay."

He sipped his coffee and smiled at me, his stocking cap pulled down low. "I feel like a kid, but I can't believe I get to have a white Christmas."

"I can't believe it's summer in Australia right now. In December. That's absurd. What do you do for a summer Christmas?"

"Well, I haven't done much the last few years, since Liv left anyway, but when I was a kid we'd have salads and barbequed meat. Kids would play cricket in the park, or we'd go to the beach. I remember getting a Slip 'N Slide for Christmas when I was about eight and it was the best present ever."

"Those sound like happy memories."

"They are," he replied. "I had a pretty great childhood. Very nuclear family, suburbs, riding our pushbikes to school, that kind of thing. It wasn't until I was a bit older that things weren't great. My parents weren't too happy that their only son liked boys. I mean, they knew and they never kicked me out or anything, but they never really warmed to the idea."

"That must have been hard."

He nodded and afforded me a small smile. "It wasn't easy. Pretty sure my dad thought it was just a phase and I'd eventually wake up to myself. But honestly, I dressed up as a different Disney princess for book week at primary school every year, I had a pet bird who I insisted be called Cher, and I would wrap T-shirts around my head and pretend I had long hair. There was no way he could've thought it was a phase."

I smiled for a brief moment but then met his eyes. "And when they died?"

He sighed. "We never really cleared the air. I mean, things were okay between us and I'd like to think that if one day I brought home a guy to meet them, they would have welcomed him. But we'll never know." He chewed on his bottom lip and studied the trees for a bit. "They had a car accident. You think you have time to sort that stuff out, but you don't . . ."

I nodded, because I understood that. "My dad went to bed feeling sick. When he didn't show up for work in the morning, I went to his place and found him. Still in bed, peaceful as ever. Looked like he was sleeping. He'd had heart failure."

"You found him?" he asked quietly. I nodded. "Oh God, Ren, I'm so sorry."

"As it turned out, he'd had some heart issues for a while. Never told anyone. The doc said my dad never wanted anyone to worry. So typical that stubborn men of that generation don't want to talk about health stuff. It could have saved his life if he'd just talked about it. If we knew."

"So true."

"I could have taken him to see a specialist." Now it was my turn to sigh. "He would have gone kicking and screaming the whole way, but I could have tried."

"Could-haves and should-haves are the hardest parts of hindsight."

I met his eyes and gave a nod. "They sure are. Sorry for making you dredge up all this stuff. I'm still trying to get used to it. I half expect the phone to ring any minute and to hear his voice."

"And you will for a while."

"Does it get any easier?"

He didn't answer for a bit. "Not really. You just learn how to live with it."

God, it felt like my heart weighed a ton.

We were both quiet for a bit, but then he nudged me with his shoulder. "Can I ask you something?"

"Sure."

"You didn't put up Christmas decorations."

It wasn't a question, but it really kind of was. "I didn't feel it this year," I admitted. "It was just gonna be me this Christmas. And it all seemed more work than what it was worth."

He nodded slowly and was quiet again for a bit. "I get that. To be honest, I didn't put anything up this year because I was leaving, and I know my sister will have gone overboard for when I get there. But if you wanted me to help you to put up a few things, I could. I'm not very good at cooking, but Christmas decorations I can do."

I found myself beginning to smile. "I have missed it, not gonna lie. It's the holidays and I didn't feel like celebrating. Being alone and all. But . . ."

"But now you're not alone," he finished.

Well, not for one more day, I thought. But I didn't say that out loud. "If you wanted to pick out a tree," I said, nodding to the tree line.

His eyes went wide and his smile became a grin. "Like a real tree?"

I laughed. "Well, yeah. What other kind is there?"

"Ah, plastic fake trees. That's all we ever had."

"You don't have real trees?"

"Well, in Australia we have real trees, sure." He rolled his eyes. "But not as Christmas trees. I mean, I'm sure some people might, but generally no. Plus, it's forty degrees Celsius and we tend to have bitey things that live in our trees. So unless you consider snakes and spiders to be tinsel and ornaments . . ."

"God no. I see your point." I shuddered at the thought. "So, is it true that all the animals there want to kill you?"

"They probably want to, but some can't. Like their teeth aren't big enough. But can we just talk about how you guys have bears? Because we don't have them in Australia, and bears terrify me."

I burst out laughing. "Well, you're lucky they're all asleep right now."

He looked around at the trees and toward the garage. "Do you have them around here? When they're not sleeping?"

"I've seen a bear like five times in my whole life," I admitted. "They don't bother humans too much. They just go about their business."

He made a face and shook his head. "Not a fan."

I don't know why he made me laugh and smile so much, but now he'd mentioned putting up a tree, I wanted to do it more than anything. "Come on, let's go pick a tree."

I trudged through the snow toward the far side of the house where the trees were closer. Hamish, of course, took five steps and almost fell twice, so I held out my hand. I had meant for him to pass me his coffee mug, but he slipped his hand into mine like it was the most natural thing in the world. It made my heart thump against my ribs and I almost didn't have the heart to tell him . . . but he was going to fall. "Oh, I meant for you to give me your cup."

"Oh!" He barked out a laugh, his blush matching the pink of his hat and coat. But he passed me his now-empty coffee mug, and I set both our cups on the edge of the porch.

But then, because I didn't want him to be embarrassed, I held out my now-empty hand. Okay, who was I kidding? I reached out for him because now I actually wanted to hold his hand, because it felt really fucking good. He smiled, shy this time, and gave me his hand. For real this time. And together, we trudged toward the trees.

There were quite a few different types of trees on my property; some weren't Christmas tree-worthy at all. But there were some balsam firs, which were perfect. "Do you want big or small?" he asked. "I mean, we all know the truth about that universal question, but if we're talking about trees . . . And where do you want to put it?"

I laughed again, scaring some poor bird in a nearby tree. "In the corner away from the fire," I said. "I'll move the sofa over a bit." Then something occurred to me. "It's not like I have any presents to go underneath it. I gave Mrs Barton her Christmas gift during the week. And don't tell Chutney, but I got her a big fresh bone as her gift. But it's in the fridge. I'm not putting that under the tree. I mean, it's not like she knows it's actually Christmas."

"You didn't buy yourself anything?" he asked.

"No, why would I do that?"

"I dunno. So you have something to unwrap."

"But I'd know what it is."

"That doesn't matter," he replied simply.

"Did you buy yourself something?"

"Yep. A plane ticket to a new life in America." He grinned. "Okay, so I didn't get myself anything this year because I was travelling and everything. But for the last few years, sure I did. When Liv was gone and it was just me. And the best part is that I know exactly what I need and really wanted. Like my Gucci boots. Best gift I ever got."

I laughed again and squeezed his hand. "Well, next year I'll have to get myself something."

"If that market place is still open when we go back for my car, I'm totally buying you something."

"From the Home Market?" I asked, trying not to laugh. "About all you're gonna get from there the day before Christmas Eve is a can of beans. If you want to wrap up a can of beans for me, you can just take one from my cupboard. Save you the trip."

He grinned. "Economical and practical. I like it. But are we talking green beans or legume-type beans, like cannellini or a black bean? Because I think you're worth more than a can of those."

I barked out a laugh. "I'm glad to hear that. Pray tell, what kind of bean am I?"

"Oh, you're the good stuff. Like edamame."

"Like what?"

"Edamame. You know, the delicious green bean things they serve at Japanese restaurants. I don't think they come in a can though."

"I've never had Japanese."

He gasped, genuinely horrified. "Oh, we need to remedy that."

I chuckled, liking how much that sounded like a promise. "Well, I don't think we'll find Japanese beans at the Home Market."

Then he gasped again, louder this time, and he

squeezed my hand. "No! I know what kind of bean you are."

"Oh, God."

"Close, but not quite." He beamed. "You're a coffee bean. Most prized bean in all the world. Or maybe that's vanilla. I don't know. But coffee. That's the one. I'm going to get you a can of coffee beans."

I laughed at how ludicrous this conversation was and loving every minute of it. "But now it won't be a surprise."

He deflated a little. "True. What if I take several cans of random things, take the labels off them? Then it'll be a surprise every time you open one."

I laughed and shook my head. "Did you want to choose a tree before we freeze to death?"

"Oh, yes," he said, turning back to look at the trees, then he turned to me. "Is it fair to cut them down? I mean, this one's cute but he's just starting out. What if he could grow to be really big?"

Oh, good Lord. I couldn't help but laugh. "Most of these will be felled at some point. It's where I get my firewood from. The smaller trees at the back of the property are the ones I've replanted."

"Oh." He frowned and turned back to the trees. He studied them for a bit, then pointed to one in particular. "Well, what about that little one over there. He's kind of crowded by the bigger trees, so chances are he won't get to grow much."

I could not believe he was concerned about the welfare of the little trees. It was funny and sweet in a way, but I wasn't surprised. Funny, sweet, and a little bit quirky just about summed Hamish up.

He stayed by the house with Chutney while I cut down the tree, telling her all about what I was doing. I couldn't make out everything he said, but he pointed and she listened, her ears up and tongue lolling out as if she understood every word.

And so help me, it made my heart skip a beat or two.

But I was excited for the tree now that I'd decided I was having one. By the time I'd dragged out all the Christmas decorations and got the tree stand all set up, we were thawed out, our boots were drying by the door, and Hamish had my fluffy socks on again. We ate some sandwiches on the couch, Hamish had his legs all tucked up under himself, and he nodded to the TV. "You mentioned you were going to watch movies."

"I had planned to," I said after I swallowed my mouthful. "But that was only to pass the time. I thought I was spending my three days off work all by myself. I have some books and a few old puzzles too. And I was absolutely going to binge-watch something on Netflix."

"We could watch the cheesiest Christmas movies?" he said. "Or we could watch something not at all Christmassy if you'd rather not. The sport channel, even." He said sport like the word tasted bad.

I chuckled. "Not a fan?"

"Some sport, yes. If there are men in tight uniforms, there's a chance I'd interested."

"Same," I said with a smile. "But if we're going to put up Christmas decorations, we should probably watch the cheesiest Christmas movies ever."

He clapped his hands together and did a little wiggle on the couch. "Great answer."

I laughed as I finished my sandwich and offered the remote to Hamish so he could choose the movie. He found *The Muppet Christmas Carol* and couldn't hit play fast enough and then turned his attention to the tree.

How my Christmas had gone from a quiet, lonely non-event to a sweet and fun, not-lonely-at-all-event, with this cute Aussie guy who had literally crashed into my life, I had no clue. But one thing I knew for sure . . . Santa Claus might have given me the best gift ever.

CHAPTER SEVEN

HAMISH

REN SAT the two big boxes of Christmas decorations he pulled down from his attic in front of the couch. I didn't want to go through them like it was a bargain bin at a Gucci sale . . . Okay, that's exactly what I wanted to do. But realising there could very well be family heirlooms or sentimental ornaments in the boxes, and given this was Ren's first Christmas without his dad, I had to tread carefully. He wasn't just opening up boxes of decorations. He was about to open up boxes of memories.

"This box is for the tree," he said, sliding it between us.

I put my hand atop it and looked him in the eye. "Are you sure you're okay to do this?"

He nodded and gave me a kind smile. "If you weren't here . . . well, if you weren't here, I wouldn't be doing this. But you're right. I should do this. I need to. And having you here helps."

I slid my hand over his and gave his fingers a squeeze. "If you want to tell me about each ornament, whatever memories you have, I won't mind one bit."

He sighed with a smile. "Most of them I bought at the store."

"You never did the family tradition thing with ornaments?"

He shook his head and opened the box. The first ornament I pulled out was a bunch of ice-block sticks glued into a star shape, covered with red and green glitter, with a pipe-cleaner glued in a loop. And glued badly, I might add. "Did you pay actual money for this?"

Ren laughed. "Hey, I made that! In kindergarten." He took it and stared at it for a long moment. "Dad kept it. He kept all the ones I made at school. This was the first."

"Then it should be first to go on the tree."

Ren's face lit up and he hung the ornament pride of place in the middle of the tree. We hung more ornaments and tinsel, then we added the fairy lights, and Ren told me stories of growing up. How it was really only ever the two of them, just him and his dad, and how his dad made a lot of his gifts when he was really young. Wooden trucks and spaceships, a farmhouse with hand-carved animals, and I was reminded that Ren was a third-generation hardware store owner.

"Do you make stuff like that?" I asked.

"Nah, not really. Not like Dad did. I never really had a need to." Ren smiled now as he talked of his father, and I hoped he found it cathartic instead of painful. "He was handy around the house, of course. Could fix anything. But building stuff was his hobby. He loved it. Model planes and ships. Whereas I do more home-renovating and building than him. Dad always said I should have been a carpenter."

"You fixed up a lot of this house?"

"Sure. It was barely standing when I bought it."

"No way."

He nodded. "It's taken me five years. Still have to redo the kitchen, and I'd planned to do it this year, but I've been busy . . . with everything."

"You'll get there," I said. "And anyway, your home is gorgeous."

"Thanks."

Pulling on Ren's arm, I stood us back from the tree to inspect our work. "We have to stand back to appreciate it."

It didn't look like any kind of tree in a department store or in some fancy magazine. The tree itself was kinda short and a bit lopsided, but it was now full of mismatched decorations that told the story of Ren's life.

It was perfect.

"I love it," I said.

When I looked up at Ren, he was smiling at me. "It's amazing."

It made my stomach swoop and my heart swell. "Now for everything else. We don't have to go overboard with house decorations. I've already tortured you enough with the tree."

He chuckled. "I wouldn't call it torture."

Ren opened the next box and the door wreath was on top. He hung it on the front door and I pulled out two old, small wooden figurines. One was a reindeer and the other was a Santa, each was about the size of my hand, and they reminded me a little of the Nutcracker. They were varnished but only had a bit of colour. Santa's coat was painted red, of course, his beard white. The reindeer's nose was red as well; his little feet were painted black.

They were old, and I didn't have to guess that Ren's dad had made these. "Oh my God, these are beautiful," I whispered. Ren stood beside me and took the little Santa.

"I think he made these for my first Christmas," he

murmured. He studied the figurine a while, his face thoughtful. "I packed them away last year not knowing it would be my last Christmas with him. I guess we don't know these things. Otherwise, I probably would have made a bigger deal out of it."

"How did you spend it?"

He shrugged. "We just hung out. I mean, we were always kind of low-key, but we'd do a lazy breakfast. We had pancakes, from what I remember. Then we had a huge lunch with ham and potatoes, and he'd make Grandma's gravy. We were always too full to eat dinner." He smiled at that. "And after we got the kitchen all cleaned up, we'd mess it all up again and bake Christmas cookies in the afternoon. That's what we'd eat for dinner."

"You ate cookies for dinner?"

He nodded, a little teary. "Every year. We'd watch whatever Christmas movie was on TV, drink hot chocolate, and eat as many cookies as we could fit in."

"Oh, Ren. That sounds amazing." I rubbed his back. "We could make cookies this afternoon," I suggested. "If you want to, that is."

His eyes met mine. "Really? You'd want to do that?"

"Uh, yes," I replied seriously. "Though a word of warning, my baking skills are on par with my general cooking skills, which isn't great. But my eating skills are exceptional."

He finally smiled. "I'd really like that." He took the little Rudolph I was holding and put him and Santa on the side of the mantlepiece. "Okay, what else is in that box?"

Next was a garland type thing that he put on his small dining table, and there were some more figurines and smaller Christmas trees he put around his living room and a runner of fairy lights he put over the fireplace. It was just enough to be tasteful and pretty without looking like a dollar store exploded.

The place looked like a dream.

Ren stood back and smiled. "I'm so glad you convinced me to do this," he said. "I would have regretted not doing it."

God, he looked so sad. All this talk of his dad was so hard on him. I contemplated not asking, but back when I lost my parents, I knew how much it meant to me . . . "Do you need a hug? Or would that be weird?"

He barked out a teary laugh. "A hug sounds great."

I pulled him in and wrapped my arms around his waist. His arms went around my shoulders and my head fit perfectly into the crook of his neck. Like, perfectly. We were a perfect hug-match. He sighed against me and I knew then that he'd been touch starved, and hell, maybe I had been too.

Because he didn't pull away and I sure as hell wasn't about to either.

I could have stayed right there in his arms forever.

He was strong and he smelled divine. The rise and fall of his breaths synced with mine, and I closed my eyes and relaxed into him. I rubbed his back and he sighed again. "Feel better?" I whispered.

"Mm," he mumbled, nodding against the side of my head.

I wanted to pull back just enough so I could look up into his gorgeous face and stare into those deep blue eyes. But I knew if I did, I'd want to kiss him, and I didn't want to ruin this. He needed consoling after dealing with emotional shit. He didn't need me coming onto him like a sex-deprived leech.

But then he pulled back, just far enough to look into my eyes. His gaze flickered to my lips and back up again, and holy shit . . . he was going to kiss me. He was so close, and his lips parted—

And then the FaceTime app on my phone began to chime. *Because of course it did.* "Dammit," I said, fishing my phone out of my pocket. It was Liv. "Sorry, I told her to FaceTime me."

Ren took a step back and let out a breath. "Sure. Yeah, of course."

"I'll just take this in my room," I said and quickly closed the door behind me. I hit Answer and waited for her face to appear. "Good timing, sis," I hissed at her.

Her smile faltered. "Sorry, what?"

I whispered as low as I could so Ren wouldn't hear. "He was just about to kiss me!"

"Wait, what?"

"I know!"

She laughed. "I'm sorry. But it's so good to see you!"

I sighed dramatically and plonked down on the bed. Her dark hair was in long waves, her dark eyes bright and sparkling, and Lord, I missed her. "You too. You look great!"

Her smile widened. "You too. Oh my God, Hamish. What is going on with you and Mr Rescue Man?"

"Well, he offered for me to stay here another night. And we spent the last few hours putting up all his Christmas decorations while trashy Christmas movies play on the TV, and we're waiting to hear back about my car, but we're going to cook cookies this afternoon."

She squeed.

I squeed.

"Hamish!"

"I know!"

"But it's been a bit emotional for him so I hugged him,

and holy hell, my girl, the man can hug. Then he was just about to kiss me when you called and ruined everything."

Her eyes went wide. "Why did you answer me for?"

My hand went to my chest. "Don't blame me. I'm the victim here."

She laughed and put her hand to her cheek. Now her eyes glinted and her whole face looked like an anime cartoon. "You look happy."

"I am. I mean, apart from not being at your house with you. And I have no idea when or if I'll see him again after tomorrow, but I'm glad I met him. I told him I'll come visit as often as I can and we can do all the gay things together. He doesn't really get to fly his rainbow flag here by himself too much."

She quirked an eyebrow. "You'll do all the gay things together?"

I snorted. "Who knows? Maybe." I sighed. "I like him. He's such a nice guy. He's genuine. Do you know how hard it is to find that in a guy?"

She raised her hand. "I'm a heterosexual woman. So yes, I do know how hard that is."

"How's Josh, by the way?" I asked. "Is he still dreamy?"

She swooned. "Yes."

"God. I can't believe I'm going to actually meet him. You've warned him about me, right?"

Liv laughed. "I have. But he loves me, so he'll love you too."

"He's a sucker for a disaster, huh?"

She laughed, only a little offended. "I was going to say cute and funny, slightly neurotic Australians."

I sighed happily. "That too."

"So, your car?"

"Is fixable, apparently. Haven't heard if it's done yet

though. Had to wait for the rental place to approve the paperwork."

She made a face. "Well, I still haven't heard if Beartrap Road is open, so I'm assuming it's not. It'll be dark soon."

"Oh no," I whispered, putting my hand to my mouth. "I might have to stay here one more night with Mr Sexy Hallmark Movie guy."

She laughed. "Promise you'll be here tomorrow."

"I promise. Ren said he'd get me to your place tomorrow, even if he had to drive me himself."

"Is he seeing his fam for Christmas?"

I shook my head. "No. His dad passed away this year."

"Oh." She frowned. "That's so sad."

"Yeah, it's his first year without him. He has no other family. Well, not that he's mentioned."

"Tell him he can spend Christmas with us!"

"Oh, I don't know . . . he probably wouldn't be up for that."

"Or it could be everything he needs and he's too polite to ask." She did that eyebrow thing again. "I have enough food for everyone, so tell him he's more than welcome."

"He has Chutney. He can't leave her by herself."

"Bring her. We love dogs!"

I gave her a smile. "I'll ask. But I don't know if he'll say yes."

She sighed. "I can't wait to see you tomorrow. I'm so happy that you're finally here. I've been counting down the days."

"Me too."

"I'll let you get back to your Mr Sexy Hallmark man," she said with a grin. "Before he thinks you're being rude or avoiding him or something."

"Okay, I'll text you in the morning when I know what's going on. Can't wait to hug you!"

"Same!" She waved and blew me a kiss. "Love you, Hamish."

"Love you too, Liv."

The call ended and I smiled as I jumped up and went back out to find Ren. He was in his kitchen, in front of his pantry, and had an old container in his hand. "Sorry about that," I said.

"That's fine. Everything okay?"

"Oh yeah, Liv asked if we could FaceTime and I said yes. She just has the worst timing."

He put the container on the counter. "Uh, speaking of timing," he said nervously. "Robert called about your car."

"Oh, what did he say?"

"The rental company called back. Apparently, there's a clause that if the vehicle has been involved in any kind of accident, they need to have it assessed by their people and organise a replacement vehicle. They can't get you a replacement car before Christmas Day."

"I thought Robert could fix it," I said, my heart sinking. "I have to get to my sister's tomorrow. Tomorrow is Christmas Eve."

"I know," Ren said. "I can drive you. I said I would if need be."

"I can't ask you to do that."

"Honestly, Hamish. It's really not that far. And it's not like I have anything else to do. I haven't been to Mossley in a while, and it's a nice drive. I'll take Chutney and we'll have a Christmas Eve adventure."

"Or," I hedged. "You could have Christmas with us? Liv asked me to ask you. She said to bring Chutney, and there's enough food so it's no imposition. I told her you might think it's weird so it's totally fine if you'd rather not. But if you're driving me, you'll already be there. If it gets weird for you or you'd just rather go home, you can, no questions asked. I mean, I'd be disappointed, but I'd understand. I would totally get it. And honestly, I don't know if you'll get a word in edgewise with me and Liv. We have a lot of catching up to do and we're both talkers."

My phone rang in my hand, and I groaned at being interrupted again. "No one even knows me in this country," I said, answering the call. "Hello?"

It was the car rental company, filling me in on what Ren had just told me. I sat on the couch by the fire as I sorted out the particulars, and I explained there was now no point in me getting a rental car because I was stuck forty-five miles from where I was supposed to be and I was reliant on the kindness of handsome strangers to put me up and drive me around. And said handsome stranger just offered to drive me to my sister's place so any prospective rental car after Christmas would be redundant because I would already be at my destination.

Ren sat on the couch opposite me and smiled, seemingly amused at my phone voice. You know the professional phone voice that's different to your everyday voice? Especially in my line of work, I had to speak with a certain authority and confidence. I was clear and concise with the guy on the phone, reminding him of his contractual obligations, but at the end of the day, the rental company's policies weren't his fault, so I didn't want to take it out on him. When the call was over, I slid my phone onto the coffee table and groaned. "So frustrating."

"You got it all squared away?"

"Yeah, I think so. But their policy sucks. What if I'd been some little old sweet lady who didn't have a kind stranger come to her rescue? And she had to find a motel that had a vacancy for Christmas, maybe she couldn't afford a few nights at a motel. I don't want them to compensate me for anything. I just want Robert to be paid for his work, and I want them to sort out returning the vehicle to a rental depot. But what if that little old grandma didn't understand her rights? They'd have put all this back on her."

Ren was still smiling. "Your 'I mean business' voice means business."

I laughed. "In my job, confidence is half the battle. Knowing your stuff is the other half. And I read through the terms and conditions before I signed. Made the people in line behind me really happy."

He chuckled. "I bet it did."

I shrugged. "I can't help it. I'm very thorough. Do you know how many people never read the terms and conditions on anything they sign?"

Ren made a face. "Uh, maybe . . ."

"Oh my God, you're one of those people."

He laughed at my outright indignation. "I will read the bank stuff and generally anything work-related. But who in their right mind would read the Apple or iTunes terms and conditions? No one reads those."

"Uh . . ."

"Oh my God, you're one of those people."

Now it was my turn to laugh. "Did you find what you are rifling through the pantry for?"

Ren glanced at the kitchen. "Oh yeah, I thought if we were going to bake cookies, I should look to see if I have all the ingredients."

I grinned at him. "What are your favourite kind to bake?" Then I put my hand up. "And I just want to say, if you prefer raisins over choc chips, we can't be friends anymore."

He laughed again. "Chocolate chip all the way. Though Mrs Barton makes these raisin and date cookies drizzled with chocolate, and I don't know what kind of wizardry goes on in her kitchen, because they shouldn't be good, but they are *so* good."

I chuckled. "So what kind of Christmas cookies did you use to make with your dad?"

"We'd make all kinds. Chocolate chip, lemon butter, gingerbread."

"That's awesome. Do we need to make a trip to town or do we have all the ingredients?"

"We should have enough. I don't have any chocolate chips, though, but we can make the peanut butter cookies, chocolate-peppermint ones, and simple sugar cookies. Or lemon ones, if you want."

"All of them or just one? I'm not quite up to speed on Christmas cookie etiquette, to be honest. I don't even know what a Christmas cookie is, and I've never baked biscuits before."

He snorted. "Wait, what? You don't know what a Christmas cookie is?"

"Nope. Is it just a normal cookie, but are there specifically qualifying criteria to make it to Christmas cookie?"

Ren laughed. "Well, basically it's just a normal cookie, but they're decorated in a Christmas theme. You don't bake Christmas cookies in Australia?"

"Uh, no."

He seemed genuinely surprised by this. "And you said you'd never baked biscuits before? Like biscuits and gravy?"

My lips curled as I even imagined biscuits with gravy, and then I remembered that they were something different here. "Oh no, no, there has been a grave misunderstanding. A biscuit to me is a cookie to you, and a biscuit to you is a scone to me. Although why anyone would want to have gravy with a scone is beyond me."

"Well, we don't eat that every day."

"Thank God for small mercies."

"Now I don't mind cookies or biscuits, but a huckleberry bear claw is my favourite."

"A what?"

He laughed. "Not a real bear claw. It's a sweet pastry."

"Phew."

"Carl, at the diner across from my shop, bakes them every once and a while. I will take you there one day and you can see for yourself."

That sounded like a possible date. "Fine. But just so you know, I brought some Vegemite with me to give to Liv. Happy to let you try it."

Ren looked horrified, then impersonated David Rose. "'Uh, that's a real quick no. Thanks anyway.'"

I burst out laughing. "Did you just quote *Schitt's Creek*?"

"I believe I did, yes."

We smiled at each other for a moment and I figured it was probably best if I change the subject. "Fine. So, are we baking cookies this afternoon?"

"We are," he replied with a soft smile. "I just better take Chutney out for a bathroom break. You can stay in here where it's warm."

"Want me to make you a coffee while you're out there?"

His smile became a grin. "I'd really like that, thank you." He helped Chutney into her coat and shoes, which was still the cutest thing ever. When he got to the door, he stopped with his hand on the door handle and turned to face me. "And, uh, if your offer to spend Christmas with you at your sister's still stands, I'd really like that too."

My heart did all kinds of crazy things, and I reckon my grin just about split my face. "Yeah, of course. I mean, sure. That'd be great." God, why couldn't I speak a full sentence? I swallowed hard and regrouped. "I'll let her know, and Ren?"

"Yeah."

"I'm glad you said yes."

CHAPTER EIGHT

REN

I THOUGHT I was ready to spend a Christmas by myself. Maybe I was. Maybe I wasn't. When Hamish had offered for me to join him at his sister's for Christmas, it wasn't just the idea of being not-alone that appealed to me. It was spending more time with Hamish.

I liked him.

He was funny and kind and cute as hell. He adored Chutney, and she liked him. If he had some hidden sinister side, she wouldn't cuddle up to him, right? But she bounced up on his lap every chance she got. And he spoke to her like she was the most precious thing in the world, and that meant so much to me. Because Chutney was the most precious thing in the world to me. She'd comforted me when my dad died, sat beside me, gave me someone to talk to when there was no one else. She'd consoled me when I cried; she listened to me as I spilled my broken heart.

I couldn't even fathom liking a guy who didn't love Chutney.

And I really liked him.

I was pretty sure he felt the same, if I could read him

properly. I hadn't had a great deal of experience, but I wasn't stupid. I knew enough to know. So yeah, I was pretty sure he liked me too.

And we almost kissed before. God, we were so close, his brown eyes were glittered with gold, his lips were blush-pink and looked whisper-soft, but then his sister FaceTimed him and the almost-kiss moment was lost. Would there be another one?

God, I hoped so.

Chutney finished her business and wasted no time in racing back up the steps. I followed her up and I'd no sooner pulled off my gloves and coat and slipped out of my boots than Hamish was handing me a cup of steaming coffee.

I don't know why it made me so happy that someone would ask to do something for me. It was sweet and thoughtful, and no one had done something like that for me in years. Probably ever. And boy, having someone at my house made it feel more like a home than I'd care to admit. I sipped the coffee and hummed. "This is lovely, thank you."

"You're welcome. Oh, and I told Liv you agreed to join us. She's excited."

"Are you sure it's okay to bring Chutney?"

"Absolutely. She offered before I could even ask. And I told her we were baking cookies. She said she wants us to bring some . . ." He made a face. "Okay, that's not completely true. She said to bring some if I don't make them."

I laughed. "What if we make them together? Is my input a qualifier, or are you not to touch them at all?"

He sipped his coffee with a smile. "I'm helping and she can deal with it."

"I'm sure she'll be so happy to see you, she won't even care who baked the cookies."

That earned me a huge grin. "I hope so."

I drank more of my coffee and began taking the ingredients out of the pantry. "So, I was thinking we could do three types with the ingredients that I have on hand. A peanut butter cookie, a chocolate-peppermint one, and a simple sugar cookie but decorated two different ways."

He looked scared. "That sounds really complicated. Delicious, but complicated."

"Delicious, yes. But they're pretty easy."

"Okay, I'll trust that you know what you're doing." He clapped his hands together. "Now, should I find a different Christmas movie or put on some Christmas tunes?"

"Um, music."

He grinned, tapped his phone screen a few times, and Maria Carey began to sing. "I just searched her Christmas album and hit play. It's gonna be a gay ol' cookie-making session."

I laughed, and we assembled a few of the ingredients we'd need and I turned the oven on to heat. I took down the cookbook from atop the fridge that my dad and I had always used; it was old and covered in over thirty years of flour and sticky fingerprints. "It's a bit of a mess," I said, trying to dust it off.

"I love this," Hamish said, stilling my hand. "Did you and your dad use this?"

I nodded.

"Ren, it's beautiful. There's so much history in these pages. Don't wipe it clean. Keep it like this forever." He was still holding my hand over the cookbook, and he gave it a gentle squeeze before letting go. "Leave it just like it is."

I don't know how he knew exactly the right thing to say at every turn.

"Show me which ones your dad liked," he added. "It's something gross with fruit in it, isn't it?"

I barked out a laugh. "How did you know?"

"All dads like fruit and nut stuff. Like Christmas cake or fruit trifle with sherry." He shuddered.

I stopped to look at him. "Fruit trifle with sherry? What is that?"

"That is an abomination, that's what that is. Blasphemy to the food gods." He shook his head as if even the memory tasted bad. "Cake doused in the cheapest alcohol you can buy, chopped up with fruit and jelly, all smothered in custard."

"Lord, that sounds terrible."

"It looks like the yack bucket at college, not gonna lie."

I burst out laughing. "The yack bucket? You know what? Don't tell me. I can guess that one."

He chuckled. "Okay, so show me, which were your dad's favourite?"

I turned the page at the front of the book. "Florentines."

"Fruit and nut. Guessed it."

I laughed. "And I couldn't even make them if I wanted to. I don't have half the ingredients. But honestly, they wouldn't get eaten. So let's stick with the fun ones, yes?"

"Absolutely. I'm really looking forward to this." He did a little wiggle dance. "Which ones are we making first?"

"Well, it's a bit of a cheat recipe," I explained, turning to the page in question. "For the chocolate-peppermint and the plain ones, we'll make double the recipe and halve the dough. We'll need to do the peanut butter one on its own. How about we start with the plain sugar cookies first. They're the easiest."

"Excellent. Just show me what you need me to do."

We fell into a rhythm of mixing and kneading, all while

Mariah Carey sang Christmas songs and a light dusting of snow fell outside. Hamish would ask if what he was doing was right, then he'd happily keep going. We used the cutters and made stars and Christmas trees and candy canes and set them in the oven to bake.

He did that cute bouncy-clap thing, all excited to have finished his first-ever batch of cookies. Then with the other half of dough, we halved it again and added cocoa to one half, then sprinkled crushed peppermint candy into the plain half. We flattened them out into somewhat even sheets and laid the peppermint dough onto the chocolate one, and I showed him how to roll them to make pinwheels.

It was kind of tricky and these weren't going to win any awards but it was fun, and Hamish was duly impressed. "It needs to go into the fridge for a bit," I explained, then took the first batch of cookies out of the oven. "But we can start on the peanut butter ones if you want?"

"Yes, I want."

He was all smiles as he hummed away to the music, and as we were mixing the dough together, he bumped his hip to mine. "So . . . You said yesterday that you never get to talk about gay things. What did you want to talk about?"

I could feel a blush burning from my scalp down to my toes. "Ah, nothing, really. I don't know . . . I just . . . Ugh."

I thought he might laugh at me, but of course he didn't. He turned and put his hand on my arm. "Hey, don't be embarrassed. I didn't mean to make you feel uncomfortable. I just thought you might have had pent-up opinions on things you can't really discuss with the Hartbridge folks."

I wasn't sure which direction he was heading with this conversation and I didn't want to jump in with both feet in the wrong one. "Like what?"

"Liiiiike . . ." He made a thinking face. "Every drama

and scandal on *Drag Race*. Such as why Chanteal would pair that pink taffeta with brown. What was she thinking? And that orange plaid skirt, girl, no."

I laughed. "Not one thing you just said made sense to me."

"You didn't watch it?"

"I've seen some episodes, but I never followed it."

"What kind of TV shows do you watch?"

"I don't love reality shows, sorry. I don't mind the home renovations shows, like the Property Brothers."

"Cute brothers. I see how that gets a mention."

I laughed. "And the treehouse show."

He frowned. "I don't know that one."

"They build amazing treehouses. But they're not a playhouse for kids. They're like a studio, only in a tree."

"They build tiny houses in trees?"

"Yep."

"Sounds cool. But you're definitely into the building and renovating shows. I should have guessed, given you're a third-generation hardware store man."

"Is that lame? Do I get my gay membership revoked?"

He burst out laughing. "Oh, hell no. A man who works with his hands and wears a tool belt. You just got upgraded to gold membership."

I snorted out a laugh and ignored how my cheeks burned. "I don't wear a tool belt, sorry to disappoint you. Though I could talk about *Sense 8* and *Schitt's Creek* if that helps."

He grinned at me. "*Sense 8*? Loved it. But *Schitt's Creek* . . . I've rewatched it so many times I can quote it."

"I noticed."

He put his hand to his chest and gasped and did a perfect impersonation of Moira. "'Be careful, John, lest you suffer vertigo from the dizzying heights of your moral ground.'"

I burst out laughing, but God . . . Sweet mercy, he did crazy things to me. So funny and cute, I could just kiss him.

Whether he was suddenly as nervous as me or if he was horrified by the look on my concentrating face—his thinking face was cute, mine probably looked more like constipation —but he turned abruptly to the mess on the kitchen counter. "Cookies," he said. "We were making cookies."

Right. Cookies.

We rolled the peanut butter cookie dough into little balls and popped them on the tray, crisscrossed a fork pattern on the top, then slid them into the oven. Then I took the pinwheel log of dough out of the fridge and let him do the honours of cutting them into cookie-thin slices.

"Oh my God, they're so pretty! Look at the swirls we made," he said, so excited and happy. "You're so clever to know how to do this! I would have totally made little snakes. You know how you roll Play-Doh into snakes? And then I would have coiled them around each other. It would have been a disaster."

I laughed at that. I don't think I'd laughed this much all year.

When all the pinwheels were cut and laid out on a tray, they went into the oven. "We need to put the frosting on the sugar cookies now," I said. "This is the fun part."

Hamish looked around the messy kitchen. "How about I wash up first. I don't know where anything goes, so I'll wash, you put stuff away, and we'll be done in no time."

"Deal."

It was so freaking easy. He was easy. Easy to talk to, easy to work with, easy to get along with . . . and I knew, I just knew he'd be so easy to fall in love with.

Like slipping on an icy sidewalk. Just walking along minding my own business, then all of a sudden my feet are gone from under me . . .

So freaking easy.

When the kitchen was done and all the cookies were out of the oven, we made red and green icing, sat down at my dining table together, and iced and decorated the little Christmas trees, stars, and candy cane cookies.

He was terrible at it, and when he'd iced one red star, I nodded to the star on the tree I'd made in kindergarten. "It's almost as good as mine."

He gasped again and quoted Moira Rose. "'What you said was impulsive, capricious, and melodramatic, but it was also wrong.'"

I laughed again. "Your ability to quote TV shows is impressive."

"But you get the references, so no judging, mister." He sighed happily, continuing to decorate his cookie. "I've had a lot of time to do nothing but watch TV."

That I understood. "Same."

Mariah Carey finished a while ago, Michael Bublé had a turn, and then Bing Crosby started to sing. "Oh, this was my dad's favourite."

"Want me to change it?" he asked quietly, all smiles gone now.

I shook my head and gave him a gentle nudge. "No. It's perfect."

"Like my cookie decorating."

I snorted and waved my hand like Alexis Rose. "Well, maybe not. 'But I love your enthusiasm.'"

Hamish burst out laughing. "And he hits me a return *Schitt's Creek* quote. I love it." We finished icing our cookies to Bing and then listened to Ariana's Christmas songs. It was probably one of the best days of my life. No exaggerating, no ridiculous pretence. Instead of being alone and miserable this Christmas, I was the very opposite. What was doomed to be a hard and sad few days was turning out to be wonderful.

Sure, I still missed my dad. But maybe the right people walk into your life at the right time. Or in Hamish's case, drove his car into an embankment. And I couldn't help but think maybe my dad had some part to play in sending Hamish my way this Christmas. Dad always knew how to make me happy . . .

"You okay?" Hamish asked.

My smile was genuine, my heart full. "Yep. Sure am."

WHEN THE COOKIES were all done, it was mid-afternoon, the sun was already disappearing, the wind was howling and snow was falling. We took a plate with a few of our cookies and a mug of hot cocoa each and sat on the couch by the fire. Hamish stopped the music and opted for another cheesy Hallmark Christmas movie on the TV.

"Well, this is utterly perfect," Hamish said. He had his legs curled up underneath him, his drink in both hands. "You know, I really like the snow . . . if I'm nice and warm inside and I don't have to go out in it. Or drive in it, or shovel it, or anything to do with it, really. But sitting by a fire, drinking hot chocolates, and eating the best cookies ever, really is amazing."

I chuckled. "Yeah, the no-driving thing might be an issue."

He groaned. "I'll need to buy a car. Or a ute . . . utility truck thingy like yours. I'll look after New Year's. I think

Liv has this week off work so if I need to go anywhere, she can drive me. I'm not too keen on driving in the snow again, to be honest. And I should totally weigh up the comparisons on buying something versus calling an Uber every time I need to leave the house."

"Well, I don't know if Mossley even has an Uber. There used to be a taxi service, I think. Or a city bus. But I can teach you how to drive in the snow, if you want. You'll be fine once you get the hang of it. And you managed to get yourself out of Missoula to here just fine."

"Yes, but the stop at *here* was rather sudden. And it involved screaming. Mostly by me. Okay, one hundred per cent by me, but I thought you were a bear or a serial killer, so . . ."

"Or a serial-killer bear," I added.

"Please, dear God, tell me they're not a thing."

I laughed. "As far as I know they're not."

"Thank God." He bit into a peanut butter cookie and groaned. "Oh, these are good."

I shoved a chocolate-mint one in my mouth to distract my mind from the way he groaned. "Mm, so are these."

He sipped his drink. "And thank you for the offer to teach me how to drive in snow. You're a brave man."

"Nah. I'm just used to it. And believe me, you wouldn't think I was brave if I saw a spider."

"A spider?"

"Yep." I shuddered. "I would be standing on a chair, screaming without shame."

He laughed. "Well, you're in luck. Spiders don't bother me one bit."

That didn't surprise me, given Australia was apparently full of ridiculously large and lethal ones. "Anything you're afraid of?"

"Ah, bears and serial killers. As clearly exhibited when you rescued me. With the crying and the screaming."

I chuckled and bit into another cookie. "You'd had a rough day."

He smiled at me, not looking away for a long moment. "Okay, so more on the gay talk," he began. "Who is your celebrity crush?"

I snorted. "Uh, I don't know . . ." I tried to think. "Adam Lambert?"

His eyes lit up. "Ooooh, great choice. When you were a kid, who did you crush on? Celebrity or normal person?"

"Well, every guy on *Baywatch*, and Jared Leto in *Camp Wilder* was a wake-up call."

Hamish laughed. "I bet he was. Okay, so first boyfriend?"

I made a face. "A guy by the name of Luke Haynes. Lasted maybe six months."

"Was he an arsehole?" Hamish asked, concerned.

"Nah, he just wanted me to leave Hartbridge. Told me I was too small-town for him."

"Oh, fuck that, and fuck him."

That made me laugh. "I did . . . I mean, not fuck him . . . well, I . . . God. I mean, I broke up with him."

Hamish burst out laughing. "Oh, I see. And now that you've brought that up. First sexual encounter?"

"Carter Campion. High school senior quarterback."

"No way!"

I laughed. "Oh yeah, a few of the football boys were up for it. Our team was very . . . close."

He cracked up. "You were on the team with them?"

"Yep. Those locker room showers are where we'll find some of my fondest high school memories."

He wiggled in his seat a little. "Oh, I love that. But wait, I thought you said you were the only gay kid in Hartbridge."

"Well, the only one who was out. They all moved away for college, and the only one I ever saw again was Carter. He came back a few years ago with his pretty wife and pretty kids when his great-aunt passed away. He came by the store just before closing time and asked if I wanted to hook up. Said he thought about what we did a lot, and sometimes he wished he was braver, but he could never live that life."

Hamish flinched. "Ouch."

"Yeah."

"What did you do?"

"I told him to go back to his wife. I told him I wasn't some dirty secret; I wasn't going to be part of anything he had to lie about. And I most definitely wasn't going to help him cheat on his wife." I shook my head. "I mean, that sucks for him and I'm sorry he feels trapped, but that just ain't for me. I walked him to the door, told him if he ever wanted some advice on being out and how to adjust, or if he just wanted to talk, then he could give me a call. I felt bad, but . . ."

"You did the right thing. Did you ever see him again?"

"Nope."

"Do you think about him?"

I laughed. "Nope. Not at all. Now, what about you? You've just been firing questions at me this whole time. Tell me about you?"

He sipped his hot cocoa and hummed. "Well, my current celebrity crush would have to be Chris."

"Chris who?"

"Hemsworth, Evans, and Pine."

"All three?"

Hamish shrugged in an it-is-what-it-is kinda way. "My first celebrity crush was the Beast from *Beauty and the Beast*."

"The Beast?"

He laughed and nodded. "Yep. I was probably about six when I first saw it. I think my parents bought the movie for Liv but I must have watched it a thousand times. Not only did I love Belle and I wanted to be Belle because of her yellow ballgown and her library, but also because the Beast fell in love with her."

I laughed so much I almost spilled my hot chocolate. "That's so funny!"

He waved his hand. "So yes, I knew my type was big, burly men from an early age. My first sexual encounter happened in my first year of college. I was a late bloomer compared to you, Mr high-school-football man snacking on his teammates in the lockers," he said with a grin, and it made me chuckle. "His name was Daniel Yang and he was gorgeous. I've had some boyfriends, one guy for about two years; his name was Antonio Moretti and he was a real nice guy, but in the end, we weren't what we wanted. That was two years ago, and I guess that's when Sydney lost its shine for me. Liv was already gone and everything else felt . . . suffocating. I don't know if that's the right word, but I knew I needed to leave."

"So you sold everything, packed up what was left, and got on a plane."

He gave a nod. "Yep."

"I spent eighteen months in LA," I admitted.

"Oh, when you said you spent time there and then in Canada, I just assumed it was a holiday or vacation."

I shook my head. "I followed my heart there. Met a guy who was doing cable work through the mountains. It was a six-month stint, and anyway, Benny was cute and fun, and we fell in love." I swallowed the last of my cocoa and set the empty mug on the coffee table. "But then, of course, it came time for him to leave. He couldn't stay in Hartbridge. He wouldn't stay, more to the point. His job paid good money and it seemed foolish to give that up, so he asked me to go back to LA with him. I wasn't sure. I mean, everything I've ever known was here, but Dad told me to follow my heart. He didn't want me to regret not going. So I did. And for a while it was great. We had a cute apartment, we went out all the time, and it was so different from here. But he worked away a lot, and my job at Home Depot was okay, but . . ."

"But it wasn't home."

I shook my head. "No, it wasn't. And things were great, until they weren't. I was homesick. I missed my dad, I missed the friendly faces, the slower pace. I broke Benny's heart, but I couldn't stay."

Hamish frowned. "That must have been awful."

"Yeah, it wasn't fun. That was five years ago. I came back and bought my house, like I was telling myself I was staying. I haven't seen anyone since then. Which is probably the gay equivalent of eternity."

He smiled at that. "You have to do what's right for you. Other people's expectations are a load of horseshit."

I stared at the fire for a long while because staring at Hamish would probably unravel me. "I was resigned to being alone forever," I admitted. "Once I came back here, I knew I'd never leave. Not for long, anyway. This was my home and it felt like I had to choose. I mean, I did choose. I chose Hartbridge over love."

"But you didn't just choose Hartbridge," Hamish said quietly. "You chose your dad, your family business, your friends. People who know your name, who ask how your day is and actually care to hear your reply. Finding a place not to call home, but a place that actually feels like home is a privilege."

I looked at him then, thankful he was on the other couch or I'm sure I would have kissed him right then and there. "Exactly," I whispered.

"So you thought being alone was the going exchange rate for coming home?"

I nodded slowly. "I just figured finding someone wasn't an option for me, and I was okay with that. I have my store, my house, Chutney. I'm busy enough." And even as I was speaking, I could hear myself trying to justify all the reasons I'd convinced myself of.

"You don't sound so sure," Hamish said.

"I was sure. Two days ago I would have sworn I was absolutely certain. It was the going exchange rate and I'd made my peace with that a long time ago."

"And now?"

I sighed. "Now I don't know." I collected his plate and mug along with mine and took them to the sink. It was easier if I didn't look at him. "I've liked having you here. And I just mean the company," I added quickly. "Not just you specifically, so don't freak out and think I'm being a weirdo because I've known you for about a day, and I'm not saying I want you to stay here, I'm just saying maybe having someone around wouldn't be terrible."

When I turned around, he was right there, barely a foot between us. "I don't think you're a weirdo. I think you're kinda great. And why shouldn't you have someone to share your life with. A guy would be damned lucky to have you. And Hartbridge is postcard picture perfect." He put his hand on my arm. "Don't close yourself off to the possibility of some lucky guy walking into your life."

Or driving off the road and into my life . . .

"I'm glad you ran your car off the road," I said.

His eyes went wide. "Gee, thanks!"

I laughed. "No, not like that. Not that you ran your car off the road, and that your plans to see your sister were pushed back a few days, and that it's been a whole disaster for you. But I'm glad you're here. I'm glad I met you. That's probably selfish as hell of me to say that, but today has been amazing. Making all those cookies was such a great way to remember my dad, and this is going to sound terrible, but I was relieved your car couldn't be fixed today. And when Robert said the road to Mossley was out, I was kinda glad." I met his eyes. "That makes me a bad and selfish person, I know. I thought I was ready to be alone, but I'm not."

He stepped in closer, put his hand on my arm, never taking his eyes from mine. "You're not a bad or selfish person, Ren. You're human. You're allowed to miss your dad and to be scared of being alone. With my car out of commission and the snowstorm, I was really stuck. I could have had a really bad time, but getting stuck with you has been great and surreal with all the decorating and baking in a Hallmark-Christmas-movie kinda way." He smiled. "So, for what it's worth, I'm glad I met you too."

My God, I wanted to kiss him so bad right then. Like every fibre of my being was screaming at me to kiss him . . . but what if I ruined what could be the beginning of something beautiful.

Hamish glanced up to the ceiling and sighed. "Except for one grossly disappointing oversight."

"What's that?" I whispered, afraid of what he might say.

He pointed upward. "No mistletoe."

Oh, sweet Lord, have mercy, he wanted me to kiss him. I slid my hand along his jaw; his beard felt amazing against my palm. He licked his lips and smiled, leaning in, and just before my lips met his, he murmured, "If my phone rings this time, I'm throwing it out for the bears."

I chuckled and tilted his chin up just a fraction, and with my heart thumping and my belly in knots, with the barest of touches, feather-light and whisper-soft, I pressed my lips to his.

CHAPTER NINE

HAMISH

YOU KNOW those movie kisses that never happen in real life? The ones that make you hold your breath and turn your knees to jelly and your insides go all warm and gooey?

I can now confirm they do indeed happen in real life.

Well, it happens in this Hallmark-Christmas-movie reality I'd crashed my car into.

Ren's lips were warm and soft, and he smelled like cookies and lumberjack. Yes, lumberjack. From when he'd cut the Christmas tree down earlier, remember? Don't ruin this for me. His hands were the perfect mix of gentle and calloused, and I'm here to tell ya, when a man holds your face to kiss you, that's the stuff of dreams right there.

He pulled back just a little, only to kiss me again, softer and his lips more open and inviting. And I honestly thought my knees were going to buckle. But we never deepened the kiss, and I wasn't even disappointed. That kiss, that first kiss, was as sweet as it was perfect, with enough heat to leave me wanting more without us tearing at each other's clothes in a sprint to get naked.

He'd just admitted to being scared and lonely, and he

was honest about me staying with him. He'd just shown me his vulnerable side; the last thing he needed was for me to start humping his leg like a rabidly horny dog.

Sure, if he wanted me to do that, I probably would. But this had that tiptoeing feeling of maybe becoming something special . . .

"I've never kissed a man with a beard before," he murmured.

I smiled, still kiss-drunk and gooey on the inside. "Did you like it?"

He thumbed my cheek and my jaw, lightly scratching my scruff. "Very much," he whispered. His gaze went from my beard to my eyes. "I'd like to kiss you again."

My breath caught and my bones turned to sponge. All I could do was nod. And this time, his hands went from my face to my neck . . . and holy shit, I thought the face-holding thing was good.

He kept the kiss sweet and tender, warm and soft. I was two seconds away from climbing him like a tree and humping him like that aforementioned rabidly horny dog when he broke the kiss just to rest his forehead on mine.

He was breathing hard, and when I opened my eyes, he looked . . . pained?

"You okay?" I managed to ask.

He nodded and let out a breathy laugh before pulling back. "I just . . . I'm trying to be a gentleman. And it's been a long time for me, so I just need a second."

Oh.

"Oh."

He laughed again, his cheeks pink. He ran his hand through his hair. "Uh, yeah. I really like you. And I want to see you again. Even if you live in Mossley. I don't want to get carried away here and now, if you know what I mean?"

I couldn't believe what I was hearing. "You want to see me again?"

He nodded. "Well, we haven't got through Christmas yet, and who knows? Maybe you won't want to stick around. Because when reality kicks in, you've been in the country for all of two days—"

I silenced him by planting a kiss on his lips. "I like this reality," I said. "It's very Hallmark Christmassy, and it honestly is the best thing ever."

Ren laughed. "So . . . you'll want to see me again? Some small-town guy who lives alone in the woods?"

"You mean a gorgeous small-town businessman who owns his own house and lives with his cute dog that has shoes and a coat, named from one of the best movies ever?" I rolled my eyes. "Uh, yes. But you're right about getting through Christmas first. You've yet to meet Liv, and we might be too much crazy for your liking."

"I'm sure she's great." He studied my eyes, then chewed on his bottom lip. "I'm so torn right now."

Well, that didn't sound good. "About what?"

He laughed again; his cheeks burned red. "Between wanting to take things slow and doing this the right way. Or . . . not."

"I'm not opposed to the *or not* option," I hedged. "Just so you know, a few minutes ago I totally had visions of tree climbing and rabid dog humping."

He blinked. "What?"

I snorted. "I wanted to climb you like a—You know what? Never mind. I think taking things slow is good. This is a Hallmark movie, after all. Gotta keep it rated PG."

Ren chuckled, then let out an almighty sigh. He took a step back, leaned against the kitchen counter, and took my hand. "It's been a long time for me, and I swore after Benny that I wouldn't do it again. But Hamish, I've known you for two days and you know me better than he ever did. I don't know if I'm saying this right . . . When I say I want to take things slow, I don't mean that we have to date for six months and get married before I give you my virtue . . ."

"Uh, I think you left your virtue at the locker room door back in high school."

He burst out laughing, and the serious mood seemed to dissipate, thankfully. "That's true. I did."

"Lucky boys."

His eyes glittered with humour and he shook his head. "It'd just be nice to take you out for dinner first, like an actual date, a few times even, before we fall into bed. Because once that starts, everything else kinda stops for a while, and I don't want to risk what could be a good thing."

I nodded and rubbed my thumb over his knuckles. "I get it. You don't have to explain. And it's sweet that you want to get to know me and don't just want me for my totally ripped body."

He chuckled again. "I do. And sure, sex is great and all, but if I had to choose between the two, I'd pick conversations and laughs, movie watching on the couch, and baking cookies."

"You don't have to choose. You can have both. If you want both, that is," I added.

"I want both."

I grinned. "Both is good. And just so you know, for full disclosure, I do *not* have a totally ripped body under all these clothes."

He laughed again. "Good. I'd rather we count how many times we laugh over good food than count carbs."

"Same. As evidenced by the cookies and hot chocolates we had earlier."

"And the pasta I was going to make for dinner."

I groaned. "I don't know how hungry I'm going to be, to be honest."

"Same. We could just have more cookies for dinner if you want? We have a few dozen to get through."

I laughed. "I'm all for more cookies for dinner, as long as there's more hot chocolate, then we can watch *The Grinch Who Stole Christmas* or *Elf*. Or our favourite episodes of *Schitt's Creek*."

"Sounds perfect. 'This is going to be just like senior year, only funner!'" he said, impersonating Elle Woods.

Chuckling, I squeezed his hand and sighed happily. "I've never been with someone I can have TV- and movie-quote conversations with before."

Ren grinned. "And I've never been with someone who knew where I got the name Chutney from."

"That's settled. We're watching *Legally Blonde*. It's not Christmassy but that's fine." I looked into those bluest of blue eyes. "And I appreciate your honesty. Before, I mean. You were honest about how you felt and what you wanted, and if it were up to me, I would never have had the courage to do that first. Even if saying goodbye to you hurt like hell."

He barked out a laugh. "Well, that's the first time I've just blurted stuff out like that. But I figured it was now or never. How often is some cute and funny Australian guy gonna run his car off the road out the front of my place?"

"I'm gonna go with once. But you never told anyone else how you felt about them?"

"Sure," he replied with a laugh. "But not two days after meeting them. And they were always a fling first, all physical and not much else. That's why I want this to be different. If that's okay with you? Because what you want is important too, obviously. It's not all about me and what I want. I mean, if you don't want to see me again, that's fine too. You did just fly into the country, and you're probably still jet-lagged—"

I booped him gently on the nose. "You're really cute when you ramble." I put my hand to his chest. "Ren, I want to see you again. And Chutney. Both of you. I want to spend more time with you and get to know you better. I don't know the logistics or how we'll make this happen, but we just need to have a little faith. Don't stress about any of that just yet. Let's just agree to possibilities."

He grinned then, with what I'm sure was relief. "To possibilities."

I leaned up on my tiptoes and kissed him. "And to eating cookies for dinner and watching *Legally Blonde* in front of the fire."

Ren's grin became something else, and his eyes softened. "Yes to all of that."

So we got comfy on the couch with our hot chocolates and another cookie each, and we opted for *Legally Blonde*. Ren turned the ceiling lights off so the Christmas lights looked amazing. I leaned against Ren and he slipped his arm over my shoulder like it was the most natural thing in the world. He was so warm and he smelled so damn good, and Chutney joined us, and it was so perfect, and I was so blissfully content, I only closed my eyes for a second . . .

"Hey, Hamish," Ren murmured in my ear. "Time for bed."

I sat up, confused and unsure of my surroundings. "Wait, what?" I stared at the TV, which was frozen on the scene where Elle Woods was wearing her courtroom outfit. "Oh, I missed the bend and snap." I frowned. "That's my favourite part."

Ren laughed and edged out from behind me on the

couch. He pulled me to my feet and led me to my room. He stood there against the doorjamb, smiling goofily. "You like the bend and snap, huh?"

"Mm," I said, still half-asleep. "Brings all the boys to my yard. Or maybe that was milkshakes. I can't remember. Ask me tomorrow."

Ren chuckled, slid his hand along my jaw, kissing me soft and sweet and warm and perfect. "Sleep well," he murmured.

I meant to step into my room but I still had hold of his shirt. "To possibilities."

Ren closed his eyes as though my words were a magic balm. He brushed his nose along mine and kissed me again, lingering and soft. "To possibilities."

I uncurled my hand from his shirt and had to make myself take a step back because in that moment, if he followed me into my room, all our good intentions would be discarded as quick as our clothes.

"Night, Ren."

He hesitated and my heart skipped a beat, but then he gave a nod and walked away. The butterflies in my belly sent a buzz of heat through my veins, and the possibility of what could be brewing between us made my heart do crazy things.

And do you know how hard it is to brush your teeth when you're smiling like the village idiot?

It's not easy. The guy in the mirror looked like a right fool. He looked decidedly happy though.

I WOKE UP BEFORE REN, which wasn't surprising because of how early I fell asleep. I guess jetlag wasn't done with me. But the sun was starting to lighten the sky, and today was the day I saw Liv. It was Christmas Eve! And I was so excited it felt like I was a kid who just woke up on Christmas Day.

I started the coffee machine and Chutney stretched in her bed by the fire. She gave a yawn as I crouched down by the fire. "Does Daddy want me to put more wood on the fire? Or let it burn out because we're leaving today?"

Chutney stood up and gave herself a little shake, then headed to the front door.

Leaving the fire to burn out, I helped her into her shoes and put her coat on, and she wiggled by the door. "Okay, okay," I whispered, pulling on my coat and boots, then my beanie and Ren's gloves, which were huge, but I realised I'd need to shovel away some snow.

The morning was cold, and when I say cold, I mean freezing, biting, bone-chilling cold. "Holy shit," I hissed, my breath coming out in huge puffs of steam.

But when the little lady needed to go, she needed to go.

So I got to shovelling. The snow was deep. Not as deep after the snowstorm but still up past my knees. And shovelling snow is hard work! But I slowly got a bit of a path made, then started on an area for Chutney to do her business.

When I'd cleared away a decent square, I leaned back on the shovel and groaned as my poor back let me know it wasn't happy. "I don't mean to hurry a princess up, and she's entitled to her privacy, but it's freezing and I should have put on proper pants. My bits are—"

"Your bits are what?"

I screamed and spun and promptly planted my arse into the bank of snow. "Oh!"

Ren laughed, all sleep rumpled and gorgeous, from the

top of the stairs. He was holding two mugs of steaming goodness. "Sorry, didn't mean to startle you."

I managed to stand up, using the snow shovel as a crutch, mind you. But I was now very wet in unpleasant places. "Holy shit, that's cold. And wet. And cold. And if my bits were cold before, they're frozen now."

"Come on," Ren said, grinning. "Get by the fire."

"I didn't know what you wanted me to do with the fire, so I just left it," I said as I trudged up the stairs, and as soon as I was inside, Ren handed me a cup of coffee. It was divine. "Mm, hot and sweet, just how I like my men. Thank you."

He laughed and so help me, his pillow-pressed hair and morning scruff might have been the sexiest thing I'd ever seen. "You decided to shovel snow for Chutney?"

"She needed to pee. I put her shoes and coat on. I swear it's minus twenty degrees out there."

Ren stared at me for a long second, smiling all cute-like. "Thank you. You warming up yet?"

I nodded. "A bit."

"You uh, probably shouldn't have shovelled snow in your PJs," he said, amused. "If you want to take them off, I'll put them through the dryer and they'll be dry before we leave."

I raised an eyebrow. "Ask every man you meet to strip out of his PJ pants?"

"Not usually, no."

"Good." I sipped my coffee. "Though I should shower and not just strip here because I'm not wearing anything underneath these."

His eyes went wide, dark and bright. "Good to know."

I didn't dare look down to his pyjama pants, because . . . well, because I didn't trust myself, that's why. I'm only human, okay? One sight of any possible half-morning-wood and any hope of taking things slow would end right here. If this was going to become some flirty game of innuendo to ratchet up sexual tension before we finally caved in, I most certainly wasn't going to complain.

He grinned and sipped his coffee as if he could see my dilemma in my eyes. "Merry Christmas Eve, by the way."

"Yes! Merry Christmas Eve to you too!" There was no point in trying to hide how excited I was. "I see Liv today!"

His smile was warm and genuine. "Why don't you go and get showered and I'll make us breakfast." He went to the kitchen. "What time did you say she could expect us?"

"No time in particular. I told her I'd text her when we were leaving."

"How about we eat, pack up, and we can hit the road."

"You want to leave that early?"

He held his coffee cup but leaned against the kitchen counter and crossed his legs at his ankles. "Hamish, the way you smiled just now when you mentioned your sister tells me all I need to know. How long did you say it's been since you've seen her?"

"Four years."

"Then yes, we should leave early. Hurry up and shower. How do you have your eggs?"

"Um, in a Cadbury's chocolate Easter egg basket, if I'm being totally honest."

Ren chuckled as he pulled out a frying pan. "Scrambled on toast, it is."

"Perfect."

I had a super quick shower and changed into my black jeans and a grey sweater. I repacked my bags and took my damp PJ pants back out. "These aren't too wet, actually," I said. "They'll dry in front of the fire in plenty of time."

Ren was putting a plate on the table and he stopped and stared at me. I was immediately self-conscious, wondering if I'd overstepped. "Is that okay if I hang them over a chair or something? If you'd rather I didn't dry my personal—"

"Oh, sure that's fine," he said, readjusting the plate on the table. "It's just . . ."

"It's just what?"

"You look great," he answered. "Very . . . handsome."

"Oh, thanks. So do you."

He looked down at himself, then at me as if I'd gone completely mad. "I'm wearing old sweatpants for pyjama pants and a long sleeve shirt that's so worn there are holes around the neck."

"And you wear them very well, I might add," I said, matter of factly. "People pay a fortune for clothes all worn and comfortable."

"I think I paid ten bucks about ten years ago. Can't say I care much for fancy clothes."

I smiled as I went to help him take things to the table. "Do me a favour and never change. The world needs more genuine, less pretence."

He carried two fresh coffees over and set them down beside the plates. I pulled out his chair this time, like he'd done for me, and he gave me a shy smile as thanks. After a few moments of eating, he asked, "So, what do you think you'll do when you first see your sister?"

"I will cry. There will be tears, so please be prepared for that. Possibly also squealing and jumping, but mostly crying."

Ren laughed. "I shall consider myself prepared."

"And then there will probably be lots of talking, mostly about people you don't know, so I'll apologise in advance for that."

"And she has a husband?"

"Yep, his name is Josh. Super nice guy. I haven't met him in person yet, but we've talked on video chat a bunch of times. They got married in a super small ceremony at the courthouse a year ago. I was going to come over for it, but then we began the plans for me to move here, so I held off."

"I'd have loved to have a sister," he said. "When I was younger, I always wanted a brother to play ball with. But as I got older, I wanted a sister. I think I'd have gotten along better with a sister."

"Well, yes and no. Liv hated that I played with her dolls and make-up, but she liked that I'd sit there for hours while she did *my* hair and make-up. And I could wear taller heels than her, she hated that, and my legs looked better. But mostly we got on okay. Better as we got older, for sure."

Ren laughed as he ate, then he sipped his coffee. "Must have been hard when she left."

"To be honest, I was so busy at work and with my own life that her going off on some overseas trip was a bit of a relief. Which sounds awful. But I'd been the grown-up after our parents died, so seeing her off on the plane was almost like one responsibility off my list. Which again, sounds awful." I shrugged. "But then she met Josh and the reality of it all hit me when she told me she wasn't coming home. I'd really taken her for granted."

"It can't have been easy," he said gently. "You were so young yourself. Being responsible for a teenager when you were so young . . . I can't imagine what that was like. I know how hard it was for me losing a parent when I was in my thirties."

"It was hard. I was at college and had to deal with organising funerals and wills and estate attorneys. I was studying finance so I was no fool, but yeah, it was a very steep learning curve. Trying to keep Liv from spiralling out of control, see that she finished high school, and make sure she didn't blow her inheritance on shit eighteen-year-olds would buy."

"She must have turned out okay."

"Yeah, she did. She had to grow up quickly too. But she got through university to be a primary school teacher, and then she got itchy feet. Wanted to travel and see the world. Someone she knew was heading to the States so she thought, why not go with them."

Ren smiled at me. "And now you're here."

"I am. I didn't get far, admittedly. Ran my car off the road on day one."

He put his fork down on his empty plate. "I'm not complaining about that," he said. Then his lips twisted in a thoughtful pout. "Do you think you'll do what your sister did?"

"What's that? Meet someone and stay here?"

There was unguarded vulnerability in his eyes, and he nodded.

My heart squeezed and my tummy tightened. "I can't say for sure. I mean, I've been here for three days and I don't have a crystal ball . . . but I gotta say, Ren, it looks promising."

CHAPTER TEN

REN

I DIDN'T WANT to sound like some needy, insecure man-baby, but I had to know. Here I was, convincing myself in my head that I wanted someone in life—I wanted Hamish in my life—and the truth was he had only been here three days, and he was here for two years and then he'd be gone and I'd be alone again.

I was setting myself up for imminent failure.

But me asking him was wrong and as I packed an overnight bag and cleaned up the house, it bothered me that I'd put him in that position. It was a shitty thing to do and I felt bad. When we were finally in the truck and on our way, I only got to the end of the driveway before I had to say something.

"I didn't mean . . . What I said before about meeting someone and staying, like your sister did, I don't want you to think I'm pressuring you into anything already," I blurted out. "We haven't even been out on an official date yet. And you've been here for three days, and I feel terrible. So, I apologise. Sorry."

He was sitting in the passenger seat with his pink coat

and hat on and with Chutney on his lap. He gave me a startled expression. "What are you sorry for? You didn't pressure me into anything." Then he frowned. "I actually thought it was sweet and it was possibly in the top three of the sweetest things someone's ever asked me." His frown deepened. "Not sure what that says about my expectations if I thought it was sweet and you felt the need to apologise."

"No, I'm sure your expectations are fine. I just wanted to apologise in case you felt pressured, that's all." I shook my head. "This isn't going how I planned."

He surprised me by chuckling. "How was it supposed to go?"

I rolled my eyes at myself. "I have no idea."

We were quiet for about a quarter of a mile, and when he finally looked over at me, he smiled. "I get it, Ren. I understand why you'd ask. You swore to never get involved with anyone again, and after just three days, you're questioning everything. Add in the fact that I'm here for just two years and you're probably wondering now whether you should get involved with me at all. Am I right?"

"One hundred per cent correct, yes."

"And I get that. Ren, I don't want to pressure you either." He sighed and smiled, offering me his hand. "How about we just see where it takes us?"

I squeezed his fingers, feeling much better now. "I like the sound of that. And thank you for understanding."

"To possibilities, remember?" he said.

"To possibilities." I drove us into Hartbridge and slowed at the intersection before the store, turning right over the bridge and following the sign that pointed to Beartrap Road.

"Oh my God, this town is so pretty," Hamish whispered. "Look, Chutney." He pointed out the window and so help me, she looked where he pointed. "Look at all that icy water. And look at all those trees by the river. It looks like a jigsaw puzzle picture." Then he looked at me. "I bet it's even prettier in the summer."

"You should see it in the spring," I said. "When everything's in flower, it's the prettiest place you've ever seen. Then again, it's pretty in the fall too. When the leaves change."

"I bet it is."

We drove for a bit longer and he continued to point out scenic points of interest to Chutney, and she continued to listen and look. From her perch on his lap, she put her little paws on the door and kept her nose to the window, both of them smiling, and it was pretty contagious.

When we got to the corner before the descent down the mountains, Hamish put his hand out to grip my arm. "Oh my God."

I immediately slowed to a stop, thinking something was wrong. "What is it?"

"Look at that," he whispered, his wide eyes fixed on the view out the windshield. This was the view from the top of the mountains before we started to wind down to the valley below, and the view was impressive.

A sea of trees and far off lands lay out before us; the forests, mountains and hills, everything was blanketed in white.

"It's beautiful," Hamish said, looking at me then, and his smile was something special.

"It is." I had to make myself look out the windshield. "Guess I'm used to the view and forgot what it's like to see it for the first time."

Hamish sighed and shook his head disbelievingly. "I can see why you love it here." Then he peered down the direction of the road. "And I cannot believe I was going to attempt to drive this road in a snowstorm in the dark!"

"It's pretty narrow in some spots," I agreed.

"And I'd rather have run off the road at your place than over that edge," he said, tapping his window. "I'd have died for sure. They'd never have found the car, let alone my body. What is that drop off the edge? Two hundred metres down?"

I had to do a quick calculation from metric. "Maybe more." I began driving again, not wanting to think of that. "This road used to be the old logger's road. It hugs the side of the mountain to the bottom."

"Well, it's pretty. But I'm glad you're driving." He gave Chutney a cuddle. "Thanks again for taking me to Liv's place. And thanks again for joining us for Christmas. I'm really glad you agreed."

"Me too. Though I feel weird about not bringing anything. It's a bit rude even, to turn up and not bring anything. Well apart from the cookies, but that doesn't feel like enough."

"You're bringing me," he replied with a smile. "Best gift ever."

I snorted. "Right."

"And the cookies are plenty good enough."

We were quiet for a few miles as Hamish continued to point things out to Chutney until she got bored and curled up on his lap for a sleep instead. But Hamish kept staring at the views, taking it all in with a real sense of wonder, and it was a comfortable silence like we didn't feel the need to fill it with anything. And when I pointed out the Welcome to Idaho sign, he grinned and buzzed with excitement.

His smile got bigger every mile we got closer to seeing

his sister, and I couldn't help but smile along with him. It was contagious. *He* was contagious.

He added Liv's address to the Maps in his phone, and all too soon, we were pulling into her street.

There were very small-town suburban, ranch-style homes with Christmas lights and wreaths on front doors, with Santa signs in front yards. I slowed down at number 164 and Hamish peered out the windshield. "Is that it? Oh my God, that's it. That's her house."

I pulled into the driveway and cut the engine just as the front door opened. A woman with long brown hair came out, trying to put on a coat, and Hamish was out the door and running. Well, kind of running. He still had Chutney tucked under one arm, his other arm was out for balance, he half-trudged, half-skipped, and slid along the path—thank God they'd shovelled or he'd have died for sure.

But he was up those front steps and hugging Liv in some kind of jumpy dance, and I could hear them both squealing and crying. Exactly like he said they would.

At least I was prepared.

I got out of the truck and closed my door, then walked around and closed Hamish's. Liv pulled back, first to inspect a squished Chutney, then she squished Hamish's cheeks. "I missed you so much! And you're finally here! And this is the cutest dog in the world!" Then she hugged him again before spotting me, still standing by the truck. She nudged Hamish. "You weren't lying when you said he was cute," she said, which I was pretty sure I wasn't supposed to hear. Then she waved me forward. "Oh my God, I need to hug you for saving my brother."

Hamish wiped the tears from his cheeks, but he was still crying. "Liv, this is Ren. Ren, my sister, Liv."

I made it up the stairs, barely, before she threw herself

at me and crushed me in a fierce hug. "Thank you so much." She sniffled. "I'm so grateful for you."

I hugged her back, trying not to be awkward. "You're welcome. It was no trouble at all."

She finally let me go and squeezed my arm. "I'm glad you decided to join us. Come on, let's get your things inside where it's warm." She turned back to Hamish. "And show me this adorable dog!"

Hamish handed Chutney over just as a guy walked out of the house, grinning. "Oh, this is Josh," Liv said. "Josh, Hamish and Ren."

"Nice to finally meet you!" Hamish said, offering a handshake.

Then it was my turn. He seemed a nice guy, with brown hair and killer dimples. "Liv's just been about beside herself," he said. "But I'm glad you finally made it."

Josh helped me and Hamish unload the truck, and we were soon ushered inside. "Here's the spare room," Liv said, leading the way. It was a spare bedroom all right . . . with one double bed. "There's just one bed," she said, trying not to smile.

Hamish shot her a glare before he went in and put his suitcase in the corner. "That's fine. We can . . ." He looked at me and cringed.

I put my bag on the floor and wheeled in his other suitcase, hoping my face wasn't as red as it felt. "It's fine, we'll be fine . . ." I took Chutney from Liv's arms. "Though I should see if this little one needs to use the bathroom."

"Here, bring her this way," Josh said. "There's some grass out back."

I put Chutney on the floor and we followed Josh back through the living room, through the kitchen to the mudroom, and out the back door. There was a large undercover area that was half deck, half grass, protected from the snow. "This is perfect," I said. "I should look at doing something like this at my place."

"It was Liv's idea," he said. "I'm just the builder of such demands. But it is great. We live out here in summertime."

I was already making mental plans for the back of my house, and for a few minutes, Josh and I discussed how I could make it work with the roof and gutters and framing it up with the fall of land. Chutney sniffed around looking for the best place to pee while we talked about building.

"Are you a builder by trade?" I asked him.

"Nah, just always something we did at my folks' place. We were always building something. How about you?"

I shook my head. "No, I own a hardware store. But same as you, we were always building something too. I'm fixing up my place right now. Done most of it, just the kitchen to go, really. But I'm sold on the idea of this." I pointed upward to the alfresco roof.

"Next project," he replied. "I gotta say, Liv has been so excited for Hamish to get here."

"He was really disappointed not to be here sooner," I said.

He smiled at Chutney. "Suppose she's gonna want a dog next."

I laughed. "Well, good luck with that." Chutney did her thing, then trotted over to me, so we went back inside, and I could finally get a proper look at their home.

There was a lovely Christmas tree in the corner, decorated with white and gold, and there were matching decorations on just about every surface. Tiny trees, garlands, wreaths, angels, pinecones, and the smell was amazing. Hamish and Liv were in the living room, sitting on the sofa, and she was holding his hand. It was so easy to see they were brother and sister. Both had pale skin, dark hair, and big brown eyes. Both of them laughed at something, though they had teary eyes.

I put Chutney down and she ran straight over to Hamish and jumped up on his lap, and he acted like it was an everyday occurrence in his life.

"Look at her shoes!" Liv said. "They're the cutest things I've ever seen."

Hamish looked at me. "Should I take her shoes off inside?"

I nodded and Liv looked from me to Hamish and put her hands to her face. "Argh! You're all just so cute!"

I laughed because they were so alike. I'd have thought maybe it was just Hamish who had that flair and spoke with a flourish, but apparently it was a family trait."

"Here," Josh said, handing me a cup of coffee, then he gave one to Hamish. He came back a second later and handed one to Liv and we sat on the sofas.

"The drive here is so pretty," Hamish said. "Everything is like a postcard, and Hartbridge is the closest thing to a Hallmark-Christmas-movie town ever to exist."

"This whole area is just gorgeous," Liv said. "But tell me, Hamish, how did you take the wrong turn-off?"

Hamish rolled his eyes and waved his hand. "'Um, it's this long, boring story involving a yacht and a famous soccer player and, like, a ton of mushrooms.'"

Liv tilted her head, totally confused, and I snorted out a laugh.

Hamish then waved his hand at me. "See? Ren gets my *Schitt's Creek* quotes." He gave me a smile before he turned back to his sister. "The real story is way more boring and involves snow, the day from hell, and an Australian guy who had never seen snow, let alone driven in it."

"I should have met you at the airport," she said.

"Well, you would have been waiting at the wrong airport because I was diverted to the wrong state, remember?"

She pouted. "Stupid snowstorm."

"Would anyone like a Christmas cookie?" I asked, standing up. I grabbed the container off the counter, took off the lid, and offered them.

"You two made these?" Liv asked. "That is the sweetest thing!"

"Well, Ren made the cookies; I made a mess." Hamish gave me a smile before he took a peanut butter cookie. "Lord knows I shouldn't have this. I've eaten so many of these cookies, Santa's giving me diabetes for Christmas."

"We can worry about diets after the holidays," Liv said. "Speaking of food. I was hoping we could do a Christmas Eve dinner tonight. Josh and I will need to go see his parents' tomorrow night. They have a big Christmas dinner. You're both invited to come, if you want, but just for us here, I was hoping you wouldn't mind if we do that tonight instead of tomorrow?"

Hamish shrugged. "I'm just happy to be here. It makes no difference to me what day we do what."

"Uh," I hedged. "That suits me. Thanks for the invite, but I'll have to leave tomorrow afternoon. I need to open the store early the day after, and I want to get up that mountain before it gets dark."

I didn't miss Hamish's frown, and apparently neither did Liv.

"Then that settles it," she said, giving Hamish's arm a squeeze. "We can have our Christmas dinner tonight with leftovers for lunch tomorrow before Ren needs to leave. I better get those rolled roasts out of the fridge. Josh, can you help me?"

They disappeared into the kitchen and Hamish studied his coffee for a second before he looked over at me. "Tomorrow, huh?"

I nodded. "Yeah, I did say that I'd have to leave."

He frowned. "I know. I know, I just . . . didn't expect it to come around so fast."

I wasn't exactly thrilled at leaving him either, but I had my store, and he had his sister. "I'm not that far away. It's just up the road, really."

"Yeah, I know. I just wish we had longer."

"But having Christmas early is always fun. We have twenty-four hours."

He finally smiled. "True. And the one bed. Honestly, I didn't know about that. I didn't even think to ask. But I can take the couch. It's the least I can do after all you've done for me."

I chewed my bottom lip for a long moment, wondering how to best say this. "Or we could both take the bed?"

He raised one eyebrow. "We could . . . though I'll be completely honest with you," he leaned in and whispered, "I don't know if I'll make Santa's Good Boy list if we do."

I chuckled at that, warmth curling in my belly. "I won't tell him if you don't."

"Ooh, a Christmas conspiracy," he said with a twinkle in his eye. "I like it. Not very Hallmark though."

"More of a Showtime Channel thing."

"Or an SBS thing," he said.

"I don't know what that is."

"Oh." He shook his head. "I don't know what the American equivalent is. We could just go with some random TV channel that shows R rated movies."

I snorted, and that warmth in my belly spread hot and delicious throughout my whole body. I hid my smile behind my coffee cup. "To possibilities."

Liv appeared, wiping her hands on a tea towel. "I have ham and a leg of lamb. A bit American, a bit Australian. Is that okay?"

Hamish and I answered in unison. "Perfect."

Liv got all teary again. "You two are just too cute."

Hamish stood up. "Can I help with anything?"

She shook her head. "No, you sit here." She took his hand, led him to the couch I was sitting on, and made him sit. "I have it all sorted. And I'm not questioning your ability to cook, Haims; I just have it all done already. All the veggies are peeled and cut, just waiting for the oven. Gravy's done. Oh, and Haims?"

"Yeah?"

She grinned. "I made pavlova for dessert."

Hamish's eyes went wide. "You did?"

She nodded and Josh appeared at her side. "Liv made that the first time she ever went to dinner with my parents. Now my parents ask her to make it every time. It's so good."

"I'm definitely getting diabetes for Christmas," Hamish said. "And fat."

I was a little lost. "What's pav . . . lo . . . I don't know what you called it, sorry."

"Pavlova," Hamish explained. "It's a soft meringue the size of a cake, topped with cream and all kinds of fruit. It's an Australian thing. Well, that's not true. I think it's actually a New Zealand thing that we claimed as our own. Like Lorde and lamingtons."

I chuckled, because honestly not much of that made sense to me, but Liv laughed, and Josh looked at me. "You'll get used to it," he said. "Most things are random and abbreviated."

Liv laughed. "Tell them what you said the other night. Tell them!"

Josh was confused for a second; then it dawned. "Oh, I said 'servo.'"

Liv snorted. "He said he was gonna duck down to the servo for some milk." She fist-pumped the air. "I got him, Haims. The conversion has begun. It only took four years."

Hamish laughed, and while I had no idea what the hell a *servo* was, I was still stuck on the comment that I'd get used to it. Which implied they just assumed I'd be around long enough to get used to it.

And I rather liked that.

Hamish put his hand on my knee. "A servo is short for a service station."

"Right," I said, not giving one rats ass about the gas station . . . because Hamish had his hand on my knee. I noticed Liv and Josh had gone back into the kitchen, leaving us alone again. "So, Haims . . ."

Hamish laughed. "She's always called me Haims. Mum and Dad called me that too. It feels a bit weird to hear her say it," he said quietly. "It's been a while since I've heard it in person."

"None of your friends back home called you that?"

He shook his head. "Nope."

"I like it. It suits you."

He smiled and rubbed my knee a little before he took his hand away. "She'd also call me Mish or Mishy when I was being an overly dramatic teenager. You know, Hay-Mish. But she'd say it 'heeeeey, Mish' or Lady Mishka, like I was drag queen."

"Because you were a dramatic drag queenager," Liv called out from the kitchen.

I tried not to laugh. "A queenager."

Hamish sighed. "I refuse to feel shame."

"'I will not feel shame about the mall pretzels,'" I quoted.

Hamish laughed and Liv gasped from the doorway. "Did you just . . ." She looked at Hamish. "Did he just quote . . ."

Hamish nodded. "Quote *Schitt's Creek*? Yes, he did. It's how we communicate. It's prettier than interpretive dance."

I nodded too. "Also, less chance of straining something and/or scaring small children," I added, making Hamish laugh.

"Holy crap," Liv said, clutching the tea towel. She did some weird eye thing with Hamish, like a silent conversation, and Hamish cleared his throat.

Josh appeared with a whisk in his hand. "What am I doing with this? And stop embarrassing them."

She took the whisk, then looked at us. "Haims, you can pop the telly on if you want. I'm sure there's something extra Christmassy on."

"We've already watched a bunch of Christmas movies and played Mariah and Bing Crosby songs," Hamish said. Liv raised an eyebrow at him, and he pursed his lips. "While we put up Christmas decorations and made cookies. I told you I landed in a freaking Hallmark movie."

"Oh," she said. "The boxes you sent over are in the bottom of the closet in your room. I just shoved them in there when they arrived. I didn't open them, so you might want to check how everything fared."

"Hm," he said. "I forgot about them. I guess I could have

a look, see what broke." He stood up from the sofa and offered me his hand. "Wanna help?"

"Sure." He pulled me to my feet and I followed him into the bedroom even though I wasn't exactly sure what I was helping him with.

He slid the closet door open and there were three decent-sized boxes stacked in the bottom. He pulled the first one out and carried it to the bed. "I shipped over some stuff I didn't want to leave behind," he explained. "Didn't make sense to bring it with me on the plane, so I began sending stuff over a few months back."

"Good idea." I looked at the box and more noticeably the return address. It was some suburb I'd never heard of, and it was weird to think of him having a whole other life in a different country. "Hamish Kenneally. 42 Wallaby Way, Sydney."

He chuckled and pulled at the tape. "That's me. Though I'm probably more Dory than Nemo." He pulled away some bubble wrap and packing bubbles, and the first thing he saw made him smile. It was another box, but this was a Christmas present, already wrapped in white-and-gold paper with a now-flattened bow. "It's for Liv," he said, trying to fix the ribbon.

There was a second smaller box, another one for Liv, and one for Josh. Hamish sighed as he pulled out two older photo albums. "These were my mum's," he said, placing them on the bed. He opened to a random page and the first photo I saw was of two dark-haired little kids in a park somewhere, laughing at the camera.

"Cute kid," I said, nodding to the photo of him and his sister.

"Mum would take so many photos," he said quietly. "It used to annoy me, but now I'm grateful." He turned to another page and there were a few photos of a young Hamish, maybe ten or eleven, with two people I could only assume were his parents. They looked all dressed up, and they looked very happy.

"That was my year-six graduation," Hamish said.

"You look like your dad."

Hamish rubbed his beard. "We Kenneally men weren't gifted with overly strong jawlines, so hence the beards."

"I like it," I whispered.

"I can't believe you've never kissed a man with a beard before." He held my gaze for a long few seconds and stepped in a little closer. "Would you like to do it again?"

"Very much," I murmured, running my thumb across his beard, scratching it just a little. I lifted his chin, so slightly, and just as I was about to bring his lips to mine, Chutney jumped onto the bed beside us.

"Oh, no you don't, little miss," I said, picking her up.

"Why do we keep getting interrupted?" Hamish asked.

I tucked Chutney under my arm and leaned down, just about to kiss him for real this time, when my phone beeped in my pocket. I groaned and stepped back, taking my phone out. "My service provider would like to wish me a Merry Christmas."

"Well, their timing sucks."

I scoffed out a laugh. "It sure does."

Hamish turned back to the box on the bed and pulled out the next thing. It was wrapped in bubble wrap and he carefully unwrapped it, and he frowned.

"Is it broken?" I asked.

"No." He pulled away the last of the protective wrap to reveal one of those wooden tic-tac-toe boards with wooden Xs and Os. "It's not broken. It . . . it was my mum's. She kept it on the coffee table and we'd play it all the time. She loved it. We didn't keep all their stuff. I mean, we kept a lot of it, and most of it was furniture and jewellery, and some of it was worth a lot . . ." He looked at the game in his hands. "But it's funny how it's the little things, the stuff that most people wouldn't look twice at, that means the most."

I put my hand on his arm. "I get it."

He nodded slowly. "Like the service counter in your store and the chair scuff mark on the office wall."

God, it made my chest ache.

"Yeah." I had to clear my throat. I nodded to the tic-tac-toe board. "Did you want to play a game?"

"Of this?" Hamish looked at the game, then to me. "You'd want to?"

I'd do anything to make him smile like that . . .

"Sure I would."

He handed me the game and he collected the wrapped gifts from the bed. I put Chutney on the floor and followed Hamish back to the living room. He placed the presents under the Christmas tree, then took his seat on the couch next to me, the game of tic-tac-toe between us.

"When I was little, we'd play naughts and crosses all the time, just on a piece of paper," he said quietly. "Then when I was about ten, Mum brought this home one day."

"Noughts and crosses," I repeated. "I like that name."

"What do you call it?"

"Tic-tac-toe."

Hamish smiled. "I like that name." He collected the circles and handed them to me. "I'm the crosses. But I will let you go first."

I chuckled and put a circle in the middle square.

"Ah, I see how you play," he said, then slid an X into a corner square.

Liv came out of the kitchen. "What are you— Oh." She gave Hamish a sad smile. "You packed that?"

He nodded. "Of course I did."

She got a little teary, but she gave me a smile. "Is he the crosses? He always had to be the crosses."

I held up one of the circles. "He sure is." Then I thought better of it. "Did you want to play?"

"No, you two can play," she replied, smiling. "Maybe later."

I slid a wooden circle into a corner square opposite Hamish's piece, and he placed an X to block my win.

I don't know how many games we played. A lot, probably. We didn't keep score, we just kept playing, game after game, laughing, and I'd pretend to get mad when he won. It might sound weird to anyone else, that two grown men would play tic-tac-toe on Christmas Eve while some Santa Claus movie played on the TV. But it was Hamish's mom's game that he used to play with her, and if playing it with him allowed him to remember her and to feel closer to her and to not miss her so much—on Christmas Eve of all days —then I'd sit with him and play it all day long.

And I'd be lying if I said I didn't enjoy it. I didn't want fancy formal family dinner parties, all for show and fake charades. I wanted stupid games and non-stop laughs and a nervous brush of fingers, listening to Liv and Josh bicker over making eggnog while some B-grade Christmas movies played for background noise. That's what I wanted.

This is exactly what I want.

"It's all a bit crazy," Hamish said, leaning back on the couch and smiling right at me. "It's not too late. If you wanted to make a run for it, you'd be home before it gets too dark."

I reached over and took his hand, threading our fingers

and getting lost in those brown eyes. "Are you kidding me? I wouldn't want to be anywhere else."

He leaned in close, a nervous smile pulled at his lips, and he closed his eyes, and—

"Haims, can you come here for a sec?" Liv called out from the kitchen.

Hamish's eyes slowly opened, our faces were barely an inch apart, and he sighed. "The universe hates me," he whispered.

"No it doesn't," I said, not wanting to miss another opportunity to kiss him, so I quickly pecked his lips.

CHAPTER ELEVEN

HAMISH

I WALKED into the kitchen and whisper-hissed to Liv. "Worst timing ever. He was just about to kiss me. Again."

Liv looked horrified. "Oh my God, I'm so sorry," she whispered back. Then she stopped and tilted her head, gripping my arm. "Are you telling me you haven't even kissed yet?"

"We have. Once or twice," I answered. "But we keep getting interrupted!"

She went back to her horrified face. "But I put you both in the same bedroom!"

"Shh," I hushed her. "I know. Thank you for that, by the way. There better not be any interruptions tonight, that's all I'm saying."

She chuckled and handed me a table centrepiece of garland and pinecones and baubles. "Can you put this on the dining table, please? And these things have to go as well."

I looked at the candles and napkins and bonbons and goblets she had on the counter. "Liv, this is all so beautiful."

"Well, it's a special Christmas," she said, giving my arm a squeeze. "I'm so glad you're here."

"Me too."

Ren appeared with Chutney, who was back in her shoes and coat. "Just gonna take her outside," he said. "Oh, do you need me to help with anything?"

"No, we've got this," I said. I gave Chutney a quick little scratch behind the ear. "Don't keep the lady waiting."

Ren grinned and disappeared out the back, and when I turned back around, Liv was staring at me. "Can we just take a second to talk about how perfect he is?"

"Imma need more than a second."

"You really like him," she stated. It wasn't a question.

There was no point in denying it; she could read me like a billboard sign, apparently. "I do. Is that crazy? I've known him for—" I checked my watch. "—oooh, three days."

Liv's face softened. "It's not crazy. When you know, you know. It's exactly that simple."

"And exactly that complicated."

"What's complicated about it?"

"He lives an hour and a half away. I've been here for three days. I don't know where I'll end up living. And I'm only here for two years."

She made a face. "I thought the same thing."

I sighed. "I like him," I whispered. "And he likes me. He's pretty heartsore right now, with the death of his dad, so I don't want things to get complicated and hurt him even more."

Liv put her hands on my shoulders. "Hamish, just go with it. If it lasts a week or a year or if it's forever, don't waste happiness. Life's too fucking short."

She was teary again, and I got thinking that maybe she wasn't talking about me. "Is everything okay?"

She nodded. "Yeah, of course," she said. She looked away then, as if maybe she wasn't being completely honest, but then she met my eyes once again. "But if you could set the table for me, that'd be great. Josh said he'd do it, but honestly—"

"And I would," Josh said. He walked in holding some kind of packing tape.

Liv gave him a sympathetic smile. "Honey, I love you, but you're very heterosexual, and I want pizzazz and perfection."

Chuckling, I gave her a nudge with my elbow. "Homosexual pizzazz and perfection, coming right up."

She laughed, and I was almost done setting everything up when Ren and Chutney came back inside. "How does it look?" I asked him.

He walked over and stood beside me, smiling. "Like something out of a magazine."

"Liv, come out and have a look," I called out. "Does it pass the gay test?"

She came out laughing, then looked at the table. "Oh, it's perfect."

"And properly pizzazzed?"

"Definitely. And I'm done in the kitchen . . . well, until the oven beeps at me."

"What else needs doing?" I asked. "If you need anything else gay-pizzazzed, I'm your man."

"Nothing," she said. "Well, not until New Year's. And I'm booking you in advance for Halloween."

I laughed. "Deal."

"Uh, Liv?" Josh yelled out. "It's done!"

"Excellent," she said, pulling out her phone. "I want to get some pics."

"Pics of what?" I asked. "Does Josh's ability to make eggnog warrant photos?"

She snorted. "No, silly. I want to get photos of you and Ren."

"What?"

"Uh . . ." Ren made a face.

I shrugged. "I was not aware of this."

Liv just laughed and shoved us in front of the Christmas tree before taking a few steps back. "Stand closer," she directed.

We muddled through some photos, which was all kinds of awkward, but I did put my arm around Ren and he slung his around my shoulder, which was nice. And remembering how I'd said earlier that Mum used to take photos a lot and how I appreciated them now, I knew in the coming days and weeks, I'd appreciate a few photos of me and Ren together.

"Now, in the kitchen doorway," Liv said, directing us. "It'll frame you beautifully."

"Okay, Steven Spielberg," I grumbled, but we did as she asked, smiling as she tapped her phone screen.

"Are we done?" I asked, still fake-smiling.

"No," she said. "Now look up."

Look up?

Ren and I both looked upward at the same time to find Josh had taped some mistletoe to the top of the doorframe.

"Rules are rules," she said, grinning behind her phone. "No interruptions this time."

Oh God.

"Liv," I said, feeling very thrown under the bus, trying to shoot lasers at her from out of my eyes.

She lowered her phone, her smile gone. "If you don't kiss under mistletoe, a Christmas angel dies rather horrifically. I don't make the rules, Hamish."

Ren chuckled beside me, his body warm from where our sides were touching. His smell filled my head, and I couldn't help but look up at him. He put his hand to my jaw, rubbing his thumb along my beard, and he tilted my face up and pressed his lips to mine.

Soft and warm, sweet and dizzying, he made my knees weak.

He held my face to his and I melted into him. My whole body flushed hot and my heart thumped hard in my chest. I wanted to do that tree-climbing thing again but kept the kiss on the PG side, given my sister was watching. I broke the kiss with a dopey smile and Ren chuckled again, his cheeks pink, his eyes glittering blue.

"Aaaaaand, you're welcome," Liv said, grinning at us. "Josh, honey, you can come out now." She winked at me. "I told him if he interrupted, he was in big trouble."

Josh came out of the kitchen and took Liv's hand. "You ready?"

She nodded.

"Ready for what?" I asked.

"Haims, take a seat for me," Liv said, leading me back to the couch. "Ren, you too." Then, while we were being seated like school kids, Liv went to the Christmas tree and picked up a small wrapped gift. It was rectangular in shape, about the size of a book. She handed it to me as if it was a ticking bomb, then quickly stood beside Josh, taking his hand. "Okay, you can open it."

"Don't we do presents after dinner?" I asked.

"Just this one," she answered. "I figured it best to get this one out of the way."

All right then. Poor Ren looked like he'd rather be anywhere else, and an impending sense of doom settled over me. "Is this bad?" I asked.

"No." Liv was almost bouncing. "Now hurry up and open it."

I slid my finger under the tape and unwrapped the paper. It was a photo frame, which I had to turn over, and the picture inside was . . . a galaxy? "Is this one of those astral charts of the date of my birth?" I asked. I thought they were bigger, to be honest. I was kinda confused.

Liv shook her head, waiting for my next guess. Josh looked at me like I was an idiot.

Ren put his arm around my back. "Uh, Hamish," he whispered. "I think it's a sonogram."

I shot him a look. "A whale song?"

He snorted. "No, that's a sonar. A sonogram, as in an ultrasound."

Ultrasound . . .

My gaze went to Liv's, and she was smiling, nodding . . .

"Ultrasound," I whispered. "For a baby?"

She nodded again and started to cry. "Twelve weeks. We can now officially tell everyone. So . . . Merry Christmas!"

"Oh my God!" I launched myself at her and Josh, crushing them in a jumpy, crying hug. I stopped jumping and pulled back, horrified. "Sorry. God, are you allowed to jump? I don't even— And I let you do all that food prep and cooking, and oh my God, Liv, you should have told me—"

She put her hand up. "And this is why I didn't tell you straight away. I knew you'd freak out. I'm not incapacitated, Haims. I'm having a baby."

"I'm not freaking out," I said, trying not to freak out. "You're having a baby! I'm going to be an uncle. Holy shit, I'm going to be an uncle." I put my hand to my fore-head. "An uncle to an actual human baby." I was suddenly hit with a wave of emotion, gratitude and love, which just happened to come pouring out my eyes. "A baby . . ."

Liv put her hand on my arm. "And here comes the freak out."

I wiped at my face, well, I tried to, almost gouging a trench in my forehead with the photo frame. Liv took the photo frame and I rubbed my stupid forehead. "I'm just so happy for you," I said. "Tell me everything! Well, not everything. I get the basics, thanks. But due date? Do you know if you're having a boy or a girl? We have so much to buy and get ready, and, oh hell yes, Liv, I have to take you to the baby section of every store we can find."

She laughed. "We'll have time for that. We're due at the end of June, and we're not going to find out if it's a boy or girl. We want to be surprised."

I nodded again, cried again, and hugged her again. "This is the best present ever."

Ren was beside me then, shaking Josh's hand and giving Liv a hug. "Congratulations," he said warmly. "Such wonderful news."

Then I gasped, putting my hand on Ren's arm. "I need to open a trust account for them for when they turn eighteen. Actually, insurance bonds are better for tax purposes—"

"And here's the finance-wiz uncle," Liv said with laugh. "Hamish, just relax."

"Finance management is very important, Olivia," I said.

She rolled her eyes. "How about we compromise, and you can start making a list of what we need to do."

She knew all my weak spots. "I love lists."

"I know you do," she replied. "Now, who wants a pre-dinner drink? And before you utter one word, Hamish Kelvin Keneally, mine is alcohol-free."

Ren raised an eyebrow. "Kelvin?"

I sighed. "It was not my grandfather's name. It's a measurement of hotness."

Liv snorted, and Ren laughed.

"Oh my God," I cried. "We need to talk names! Come and sit with me," I said, taking her hand and pulling her to the couch with me. Josh came back out with champagne flutes and Ren took his and sat on the floor, his long legs stretched out. Chutney quickly found his lap. Josh handed me and Liv our glasses and he sat on the single-seater.

"We're not telling anyone our name choices just yet," Liv said. "Sorry. But everyone has an opinion, and when Josh's sister Tilly and her husband Scott told his parents the names they had picked out, his mom made some jokes and Tilly cried for a week, and the name was ruined and she was heartbroken."

Josh nodded. "She was devastated, so we're keeping our cards pretty close right now."

I frowned at Liv. "That must have been awful for her. And I don't mind, honestly. I'll just call the baby Migaloo until you're ready to announce it, and if that's not until the baby's born, so be it. Migaloo it is."

Ren squinted at me. "Migaloo?"

I pointed to the photo frame. "For the sonar. You know, Migaloo, the famous whale."

He chuckled and raised his champagne glass. "To the parents-to-be. It's wonderful news."

I squeezed Liv's hand. "It's the best news. Though I can't believe you kept it from me all this time!"

"If you were staying in Australia, I would have told you before, but I really wanted to tell you face to face."

"You're gonna be the best mum," I said, getting teary again.

She nodded. "And you're gonna be the best uncle."

"Gay uncles are the best," I agreed. "All style and disposable income."

Ren and Josh laughed, and something beeped in the kitchen. "I'll get it," Josh said.

"It'll be the meat. Can you take them both out, please?" Liv smiled as Josh disappeared into the kitchen. "He's been wonderful," she whispered. "You should have seen his face when I told him I was pregnant, Haims. He was . . . just so in love. I can't explain it any other way."

I gave her hand another squeeze. "Good. I'd hate to have to kick his arse."

Liv snorted. "Yeah, okay, Chuck Norris, settle down."

"What? Like I couldn't. You know how many times I've seen *Mean Girls*."

Ren laughed again. "Are all conversations with you like this?"

"Mostly," Liv answered. She patted my knee. "There's nothing that can't be explained by movie quotes and song lyrics."

I chuckled. "Yep. 'And when used appropriately, it has an eighty-three per cent rate of return on a dinner invitation.'"

Liv tilted her head, not getting the reference, but Ren laughed. "'It's called the bend and snap,'" he explained while finishing the movie quote.

Liv laughed. "Oh God, you two really are perfect for each other."

She stood up and offered Ren her hand. He took it, a bit confused, and she helped him to his feet. Then she promptly shoved him onto the couch next to me. "Dinner won't be long. Do I need to get the mistletoe?"

I snorted. "No thanks. I think we're good." I met Ren's eyes. "Are we good?"

He nodded. "We're good." Then he leaned in and gave me a soft, lingering kiss that left my brain buzzing.

"Wow," I breathed.

Ren chuckled and leaned back on the couch. He reached over and took my hand, threading our fingers. "Is this okay?"

My heart was doing all kinds of crazy things, and all I could do was nod.

"I like holding hands," he murmured.

"Same." I had to swallow down some jitters. "I'm so glad you're here."

He let his head fall back on the couch, never taking his eyes from mine. "Same."

"I'm going to be an uncle," I whispered. "I can't believe it."

"It's wonderful news." He glanced at the kitchen. "Should we go help your sister?"

"Yes, we should," I replied. "But she will more than likely yell at us."

"We should risk it. Come on." He stood and pulled me up with him, but then he gestured me toward the door. "But you go first. Last time a girl yelled at me it was junior high and Felicia Martin thought it was me who pulled her bra strap, but it wasn't. Sam Oberfeld did it and he told her it was me. I was horrified, she yelled at me, rightly so, mind you. But there's some residual trauma, and now whenever a woman yells, I get cold all over. My hands go all clammy. It's weird and gross."

I chuckled. "Poor you! And poor Felicia. But not poor Sam Oberfeld. Did he get what he deserved?"

Ren raised an eyebrow. "Well, he got something."

I gasped. "Was he one of the lucky guys in the football dressing rooms?"

Ren laughed and blushed a little. "Maybe."

I gave him a nudge. "Remind me to tag along to your high school reunion. Sounds like it'd be a lot of fun."

He laughed and we helped Liv and Josh carry everything out to the table. There was ham and lamb, roast potatoes and pumpkin, beans, corn, and gravy. And it was amazing.

We turned the TV off and played a shuffled mix of Taylor, Ari, and Mariah's Christmas songs, we ate, we talked, and we laughed. Chutney slept in her bed by the fire, and snow began to fall again outside.

It was truly magical.

"This has been the best Christmas I've had in years," I said, raising my glass. "To my sister and her handsome husband, and to baby Migaloo."

Liv got all teary, Josh blushed, and Ren grinned as he tapped his glass to mine. "Cheers."

"To being together again," Liv said, raising her sparkling mineral water. Her eyes were glassy when they met mine. "To new beginnings."

Josh raised his glass. "To the family here today, and to the family we have only in our hearts."

Ren swallowed hard and nodded. "Merry Christmas."

I gave his thigh a squeeze under the table and gave him a nod. "Merry Christmas."

"Okay, enough of the mushy stuff," Liv said, wiping her eyes. "Or I'll be a blubbering mess."

"Ren and I are cleaning up after dinner," I announced, knowing Ren wouldn't mind. I nodded to both Liv and Josh. "You guys can go and put your feet up. This will be your last Christmas Eve where it's just you two, so you need to go enjoy the peace and quiet while you can."

"We still have desserts to go," Liv said.

"We'll clean this up first, then serve desserts. You two go get comfy on the couch," I said, standing up. I collected a tray of meat and headed toward the kitchen. "Now, can I get anyone anything else while I'm up?"

"Yep, you can stop right there," Ren said. He got up and walked over to where I'd stopped, thinking I'd done something wrong. He smirked and pointed upward, to the mistletoe. "Rules are rules."

I laughed and he planted a kiss on my lips, careful not to touch the tray between us. "I like this rule."

We cleared away the table and I washed up while Ren dried. "Hope you didn't mind me putting you on wash-up duty with me," I said.

"Not at all," he replied. "It's the least we could do, really."

He put the last plate on the counter while I wiped down the sink, and when I was done, he handed me the tea towel to dry my hands. Then he took it from me, real slow like, and stepped in closer, pushing me gently back against the sink. "This okay?" he murmured against my lips.

I could barely nod. Sure, he'd kissed me before, but he'd never pressed himself against me like this. My heart was in my throat, every nerve ending was alight. He felt so good against me, every part of him, his body, his strength, his warmth . . . his kiss.

My God, this man could kiss.

And this was no PG-rated kiss. It was open mouths, tongues, and hands, deep and consuming.

I'd been kissed a lot, but I'd never *ever* been kissed like that.

My eyes rolled back in my head; my knees went weak. I would have fallen over if he wasn't pressing me against the counter. When he broke the kiss, I was left breathless and wanting, drunk on him, his touch, his taste.

His lips were wet and red, his cheeks were pink, and his eyes were a sparkling blue. And he was looking at me with wonder and desire . . . I was certain I was looking at him much the same. But dammit, this man was truly something.

"Merry Christmas to me," I whispered.

Ren chuckled, warm and throaty. "And me." He sighed contentedly. "Should we offer to serve dessert?"

I gave a nod. "Yeah. Unless you just want to skip to the sharing-a-bed part."

Ren barked out a laugh and took a step back, his eyes bright with promise. "Dessert first."

I nodded, not even disappointed. We were sharing a bed later, after all. Now was the time to be with Liv and Josh, eat far too much sugar, and watch the sappiest Christmas movie we could find.

Which is exactly what we did.

We sat on the couches, me with Ren, Liv with Josh, and plates of pavlova and ice cream on our laps, and we watched Liv's choice of *It's a Wonderful Life*. We had eggnog and more Christmas cookies when the film was nearly over, and sitting all cosy with Ren, in my sister's living room, all toasty and warm while snow fell outside was a feeling I couldn't have dreamt of.

But Liv yawned, and after another hug, she and Josh went to bed. I was pretty sure she was giving Ren and me some alone time. Her subtlety could use some work, not gonna lie. Ren took Chutney out for one last bathroom break and he came back in, cheeks flush and a dusting of snow on his hair. He was grinning though, and by the time

I'd washed up our dessert plates and cups, Ren had Chutney's shoes and coat off.

And there was only one thing left to do.

"So," I began, trying not to let my nerves get the best of me. "One bed, huh?"

Ren nodded slowly. "I *can* take the couch if you'd prefer."

"I would *not* prefer that," I said quickly. "At all." Then I wondered if he wasn't too keen on the idea. "Hey, um, if it's . . . we, uh, we don't have to do anything. That's not . . . I'm okay with just sleeping. There's no pressure on either of us to do anything we're not comfortable with."

He swiped his thumb across my cheek, then scratched my beard a little. "No pressure at all. And I don't think some things would be appropriate," he whispered. "Given we're guests in your sister's house and all. But there are some things we could do . . . going straight to sleep is one of them."

"We could," I hedged. "Orrrrrr perhaps we could take the mistletoe down from the kitchen doorway and stick it to the headboard?"

Ren's grin was heart-stopping. "Then it would be a rule, right? We'd have to make out in bed."

"Exactly."

"And if that leads to something else . . . ?"

"Well, I do believe in equal opportunities," I said, very seriously. "And, as a foundation of what is fair and good for one person should therefore be readily available to all people. And I hardly think it's fair that Santa is the only one who gets to come tonight."

Ren stifled a burst of laughter. "Right. Equality and all that is important."

"I'm glad we agree." I couldn't help but smile. "But how about we start with the making-out first. No pressure."

He put his finger to my chin and tilted my face up for a quick, soft kiss. "No pressure."

I took his hand and led him to our room, closing the door quietly behind us. The room was lit by one bedside lamp, making the bed look soft and inviting. Ren cupped my face and brought me in for a kiss. A deep kiss, with a taste of tongue and promise. This was a kiss that was leading some-where. He was in charge, and I was totally on board with that.

He lifted the hem of my sweater and slowly pulled it upward. I began on the buttons on his shirt, trying to be as patient as him, and when he pulled my sweater over my head, he let his shirt fall to the floor. He made quick work of his tee, as I did with mine, and then we were both shirtless, and oh sweet heavens above . . .

He was all country boy-lumberjack under those clothes. Before I could say anything, he took my face in his hands and kissed me, harder this time. Deeper and hotter, with more urgency and desire.

He broke the kiss suddenly, resting his forehead to mine. "Oh God, Hamish."

"What's wrong?"

His eyes opened then, fierce blue. "Nothing at all. I just . . . I haven't wanted something, someone, like this in so long." He looked a little pained. "I'm trying to cool it a little."

I snuck my fingers beneath the waistband of his jeans and popped the button. "Or we could not cool it at all, and you could lay me on that bed and finish me in record time."

He grinned, with all the permission he needed, and walked me backward to the bed, kissing me, pulling at the button on my jeans. I took care of mine and he quickly pulled his jeans down, leaving only his briefs on.

And holy sweet Father Christmas, angel of large candy canes, his cock . . .

My mouth watered and my belly tightened, my own dick throbbed at the sight of him. He palmed me, and I gripped him, making his breath stutter, and he shivered. We fell onto the bed, him between my legs and his tongue in my mouth. Our cocks pressed together, through our briefs, but hot, and fucking hell, so close already.

I rolled my hips and he shuddered, thrusting against me. I slipped my hand between us, pulling his briefs away to grip him, and his eyes rolled closed. "Hamish, I . . ."

"Me too," I replied.

I slid my fingers around both of us, our shafts slick and sliding together, like silk on hot steel.

"Oh God," he breathed. "I'm . . . I . . ."

I pumped us harder, knowing he was so close. He was so big in my hand, so hot to touch. The look of ecstasy on his face, the smell of our sex in the room, and my own orgasm hit me like a freight train.

Ren's eyes opened in wonder as I came, and he followed right after me, our come spilling onto my belly and chest. He grunted low in his throat, his neck corded, and I'm telling you right now, it was the hottest, most glorious sight I'd ever seen.

Ren collapsed on top of me, shuddering and breathing hard, murmuring sweet nothings in my ear while I rubbed circles on his back. Eventually he pulled back and met my eyes. "So much for trying to make it last. I had every intention of trying to make it last."

"There's always round two?"

He grinned, heavy-lidded and gorgeous. "How about we get cleaned up first?"

"Hmm." I licked my lips. "Shower?"

He nodded and peeled himself off me, then helped me to my feet. "God, you're gorgeous," he murmured, kissing me softly.

I was covered in sticky come, my underpants were around my thighs, my softening dick was doing a great impression of Grover's nose, and I still had my socks on. Exactly like him, except his dick was more of a Snuffleupagus than a Grover. I took his hand and started for the door. "Come on, Snuffy. Shower time."

"Snuffy?"

"My favourite Muppet from *Sesame Street*." I gestured to his dick.

Ren laughed at that, and we got in the shower, all soapy and smiley, kissing and always touching. And when we climbed back into bed, under the covers this time, he was quick to pull me into his arms.

He kissed me slower this time, more tenderly, but with no less passion. He let his hands roam all over me, touching everywhere he could reach. He kissed my neck, my shoulder, my chest, my throat, behind my ear.

Every move, every touch, every kiss was so gentle, he made me feel adored, cherished. And when he rolled on top of me, I widened my legs and it felt so right, so natural. If we had condoms and lube, I'd have welcomed him inside me right then. All of him, for as long as he wanted, for whatever he needed . . .

We wouldn't be doing that tonight, but one day. I knew we would.

Tonight was more than that. Tonight was long kisses, languid tongues, safe arms and gentle hands, rolling hips.

This was tender and personal. This was us saying yes to the possibilities without having to say a word.

I could feel the emotions, taste them, and from the look in his eyes, I knew Ren could too.

And when our orgasms found us the second time, we were wrung out and exhausted, content and happy. Ren fell asleep with his arms around me, and as I was drifting off to the beat of his heart, I swear I heard jingle bells somewhere far off in the snow outside.

CHAPTER TWELVE

REN

HAMISH STIRRED AND SIGHED, his head on my chest, my arm around his shoulder. "Merry Christmas," I mumbled into his hair.

"Hmm," he hummed. "Time is it?"

"Seven."

He sighed again. "Should probably get up."

He made no move whatsoever to get up.

"Probably."

I also made no move whatsoever to get up.

I wanted to stay right there for as long as I could. I was leaving him today, with no idea as to the next time I'd see him. And just like he could read my thoughts, he snuggled into me. I held him a bit tighter. "I think Liv and Josh are up. And Chutney will need to go outside," I said eventually.

Hamish hummed. "Yeah."

I rubbed his back. "It's Christmas Day."

He looked up then, smiling sleepily at me. "Is it snowing?"

I lifted my head and tried to see out the window. "Dunno. Probably."

"If it's not snowing too much, I was thinking you and I could go for a walk after breakfast," he said. "Nowhere too far, just stretch our legs and talk."

I frowned. "Oh. Talk? As in, *the* talk . . . the 'it's not you, it's me' talk."

His smile died and he shot up, giving me a startled, horrified look. "What? No, not *that* talk. Wait, why would you think that?"

"I wasn't thinking that until you said it just now."

He screwed his face up and sat up, chuckling. He patted my chest. "No, sorry, I just thought it'd be nice. Just the two of us, oh, and Chutney, of course. Walk a block or two, depending on how frozen I am. Just to spend time together before you leave, that's all. Not the 'it's over now I've used you for your body' talk." He lifted the sheet at my chest and tried to peek underneath. "And I do have to say, it's a mighty fine body," he said with a cheeky grin before he took my hand and brought my knuckles to his lips. "Definitely not that kind of talk."

I tugged on his beard a little. "Good."

The truth was, saying goodbye to him today and heading home would be hard enough, even knowing it was probably only temporary. I would see him again. I just didn't want to leave him. It was something we would definitely need to discuss.

"You know those possibilities we talked about," I began. "Well—"

"Coffee's ready," Liv called out from what sounded like the kitchen or living room.

Hamish frowned. "Thanks!" he called back. Then his eyes met mine. "What about those possibilities we talked about?"

"You do want to see me again?" I asked, just blurting it

out, not at all how I wanted to phrase it. We had talked about this, but I needed to hear it again, even though this probably wasn't the time or place for this conversation, but it was too late now.

"Uh, yes." He looked at me as if I was crazy. "I'll take more of last night, yes, please and thank you. Actually, more of the last three days as a whole." He waved his hand in a circle. "All of it. Except for the running off the road thing, and the cry-screaming that you were a serial-killer bear. We can just skip those parts. But I'm definitely interested in—" He smiled. "In the possibilities."

It made my heart so happy to hear that. And relieved, which I'm certain he could see on my face. "Good. Same. I am too." I stopped short of asking him outright what those exact possibilities were, even though I really wanted to know, because his sister was waiting for us. Would we see each other on weekends? Every weekend? Every second weekend? Once a month? I wanted to ask but didn't want to come across as needy. "Whatever those possibilities might be."

Hamish grinned and climbed off the bed, stark naked. "Santa brought coffee, apparently." He rifled through one of his suitcases and pulled out his PJ's and quickly put them on, then stopped and stared at me. "Are you . . . did you not want breakfast? I can bring you a coffee if you want to stay in bed?"

I chuckled. "I was just enjoying the view."

His grin widened and his cheeks tinted pink. "I'll go out first. That way Liv can embarrass only me while you throw on some clothes."

"Deal."

He slipped through the door and pulled it closed, and I sighed up at the ceiling. I was happy for the first time in a long time, even with me leaving today. He wanted to see me again. We had possibilities we needed to sort out, but things were good. Actually, things were great.

Hamish was great.

Last night had been amazing. His body, his mouth, his . . . everything. But it was more than that with him. He was funny and smart and kind and sensitive and honest.

And he was waiting for me with fresh coffee . . .

I threw back the covers and pulled on my jeans and a shirt, then detoured to the bathroom before venturing out to the kitchen. Liv had some Christmas piano music playing and the house was warm, and something smelled amazing. I poked my head into the kitchen.

"Oh, here you are," Hamish said, handing me a coffee. "Josh is cooking pancakes for breakfast."

"Merry Christmas, Ren," Liv said. Her hair was in a messy bun; she wore flannel pyjamas and a huge smile. "Sleep well?"

I got the distinct impression that in the thirty seconds of my absence that Hamish had told her everything we'd done last night. I sipped my coffee, pretending I wasn't embarrassed. "Slept really well, thank you." Chutney was, of course, by my feet. "I better take this little one out for a bathroom break."

"I'll get her shoes," Hamish said, disappearing out to the living room. He tied on her four little shoes while I held her.

"Awww," Liv said. "You're just so cute together." Hamish shot her a please-shut-up glare, but she rolled her eyes. "I can't help it. I'm hormonal and clucky."

I laughed as I took Chutney out back, and in no time at all we were sitting down eating a breakfast of pancakes and bacon and fruit, more coffee and juice, and listening to Christmas songs on the TV. There was a decent foot of snow on the ground, but the sun was out and it really was a perfect Christmas morning.

When we were done eating, Josh disappeared from the table and he came back out push-sliding a huge box. It was covered in Christmas wrapping so we couldn't see what was in it, but his grin was huge. "Now, I know we said no expensive gifts this year because of the baby and all," he said, looking mightily pleased with himself. "But I couldn't resist."

Liv stood up. "Is that for me?"

He shrugged. "Well, yes and no. It's for us . . . as a family."

She put her hand to her mouth. "Josh, what did you buy?"

"Come and open it," he said, grinning.

Liv tore into the paper, and as soon as she saw what it was, she stood back and began to sob. "You said it was too expensive."

He wrapped her up in his arms. "But I saw how much you loved it, so I went back. I had to go pick it up from Mom and Dad's yesterday."

Liv wiped at her eyes and turned the box around so we could see it was a fancy looking crib.

"And there's a matching changing table too," Josh added. "We just have to assemble them. And then we can start decorating the baby's room."

And of course, Liv began to cry again. "I don't know why I'm crying," she sobbed.

"Because hormones are horrible," Josh whispered. "Can I make you some hot chocolate?"

She nodded and sat down on the couch and pulled the crib box over, pulling at the wrapping paper.

"It's so beautiful," she said, looking at me and Hamish.

"We saw it in a store but it was really expensive."

Hamish went over to her and put his arm around her. "Josh adores you," he said. "I can see why you moved half a world away for him."

She nodded and wiped her snotty face with the back of her hand. "Who knows, you might find someone worth moving half a world away for too?" she said, glancing at me.

Oh, okay, wow.

Hamish laughed, blushing bright red. "No pressure at all," he said, then mouthed *sorry* at me.

The thing was, I didn't really mind.

"Here, let me get you my present," Hamish said instead. He shot up and collected one of the boxes he'd put under the tree, and he handed it to Liv.

She unwrapped it and opened the box, and this time, she squealed with delight. She pulled out an assortment of candies, crisps, crackers, and a black-and-yellow tube. "Oh, hell yes," she said.

Josh appeared, carrying a mug of fresh hot chocolate. He saw what she was holding and he stopped. "Oh no."

Hamish laughed. "There's a few tubes. Easier to bring over than the big jars."

Liv turned it around to show me. Vegemite.

"That shit is nasty," Josh said.

"Our baby will be raised on it," Liv said proudly. She unscrewed the cap and squeezed a small amount onto her finger and tasted it. "Oh, I've missed this."

Hamish grinned. "And there's Chicken Crimpies, Violet Crumbles, Smith's chips, Twisties, Maltesers, and whatever else I could find."

Liv hugged him. "It's perfect, thank you."

Hamish collected the other two gifts he'd brought with

him and handed one to Josh and the other Liv. "These are just a little something from home."

They took their gifts and began to open them, and Hamish came back and sat on my lap. "I'm sorry I don't have anything for you. We didn't go to the Home Market to get you that can of beans."

I chuckled. "I don't need anything," I said. "Being here is enough."

He leaned down and kissed me. "Merry Christmas, Ren."

"Merry Christmas, Haims."

He grinned and wiggled his bony ass on my legs. "Ow."

He laughed and Liv pulled out a hoodie, which she hugged and cried over, and Josh put his new matching cap on his head. They appeared to be of some red-and-white sporting team, presumably Australian. "Love it, thank you," Liv said.

"I tried to think of the most Australian things I could get you," Hamish said, still on my lap. "Without looking like a *Crocodile Dundee* parody."

Liv laughed. "And your gift," she said, handing Hamish a box. He made no effort to move from my lap, and I was quite content to let him sit there. He opened the box and pulled out some thermal underwear and socks. "Oh my God, I need these!" he cried. "Now I can give Ren back his."

Liv and Josh both looked at me, and I laughed. "Very genuinely don't want them back."

"I knew you wouldn't be prepared," Liv said. "There's some gloves in there too."

"I'm going to have to go shopping for a lot," Hamish replied. "Boots. I need proper boots that aren't Gucci, apparently. Then I can give Ren back the ones I borrowed."

"I don't mind," I offered gently, giving him a squeeze. Then I mumbled into his shoulder, "How about we clean up the breakfast mess?"

"Good idea." He put the box on the table, gave his sister another hug, then we cleared the table. We cleaned everything up and Josh and Liv had begun to pull the crib pieces out of the box, Hamish declared that he, Chutney, and I were going for a walk.

Boots and coats on the three of us, Hamish pulled on his stocking cap, the pink one that matched his coat, and smiled at me. "We all ready?"

I grinned at him as I put my own hat on. "Yes, sir."

So out we went, and Hamish got as far as the porch. "Oh, holy shit."

"What's wrong?" I asked, fixing Chutney's lead.

"It's freezing," he breathed, plumes of steam for breath.

"Yep. Not sure how long Chutney will be out here for, to be honest."

Hamish gasped. "Is she cold? Even with her coat and shoes on? Ren!"

"She's fine. It won't hurt her to walk for a bit."

"She was running around like crazy through the house all morning!" He looked genuinely horrified and quickly picked her up. "No, pretty baby, come here." He unzipped his coat and stuffed her inside, zipping it back up so her little face peeked out the top. She grinned, Hamish grinned, and all I could do was smile.

"Come on then," I said, walking down the steps and along the driveway. Hamish walked like he was on the moon, which made me laugh, so I took his hand, and by the time we got to the sidewalk, he found his stride. Kind of.

"It really is beautiful," he said.

"The snow?"

"Yeah. I mean, it's frighteningly cold, and how people live in this by choice is baffling. But it's pretty, and peaceful. I guess it's still new to me."

"Well, it is pretty," I replied. "But after you have to shovel it for hours and you can't just duck into the store or you're stuck at home for days and you have to worry about water pipes freezing, then it's not so beautiful."

"You're not doing a very good job of selling it to me. You're supposed to be upselling it and telling me it's the best place to live."

I chuckled. "Right. I forgot, sorry. Yes, shovelling six feet of snow is so much fun!"

"Six feet of it?" He looked stricken.

That made me laugh. "But the ice skating is romantic, and the wood fires and hot chocolate are amazing, and there is nothing in the world better than being in bed on a lazy Sunday while snow falls outside. Making love for hours . . ."

Hamish stopped walking. "Okay, sold."

"That was fast."

"You're a good salesman. You know your target market, and this audience of one is intrigued."

I chuckled again. "Honestly, I'm not selling anything. Shovelling snow sucks, but truly, it's worth it. Come spring and summer, there's no place prettier in all of the world."

Just then, two small kids came out of the house we'd stopped in front of. "Merry Christmas," they yelled and waved.

"Merry Christmas," I called back, and Hamish gave them a friendly wave.

"Did Santa visit you?" the little girl asked.

"He sure did," Hamish replied, glancing at me.

The mom came out then and ushered her kids back

inside, waving to us and wishing us a Merry Christmas before she closed the door.

Hamish sighed. "This all still feels like a Hallmark Christmas movie."

"Is that so bad?" I asked.

He squeezed my hand. "Not at all. It's perfect, actually. I don't want it to end."

"It doesn't have to end, does it?" I asked, ignoring my hammering heart. "When I go back to Hartbridge, we'll see each other again, right? On weekends?"

"Yes, please. On weekends, or if I can bring my work laptop, I could come up during the week. If you want. I don't have to stay with you," he said quickly. "If that's too much. I can stay at the motel in town if they're not busy with the holiday rush, and I didn't mean to just invite myself to stay with you—"

Chutney licked his face and it made me laugh. "I think she's trying to tell you something."

He shuffled her inside his coat so she couldn't lick his face anymore. "What's she telling me? That I talk too much or that I need a face-licking?"

I took his hand. "That you can stay with us. That she'd be disappointed if you didn't . . . that *I'd* be disappointed if you didn't stay with us."

He grinned, but then he made a face and looked down the street. He was quiet a moment and I gave him the time he needed to get his thoughts in order. "I don't want to sound like some crazy person or some psycho-weirdo, so please don't think that, but I just need to say this or I'll drive myself insane wondering if I should have."

"What's that?"

He swallowed hard and met my eyes. "I like you. Like, I *really* like you. And I've known you for all of three and a half days, which is where the psycho-weirdo thing comes in because you know when you see those shows where some person says, 'yeah, they ran away to meet some person they met three days ago and that's why we're on an episode of *Australia's Most Wanted*' because who the hell thinks they even know someone after just three days, but . . ." He sighed. "But I think I *do* know you. Not overly well, admittedly, and I'm sure you have some lurking behavioural traits that might possibly drive me mad, which is not a bad thing because just you wait to find out mine. But I know you saved me, and you looked after me. I know how you get sad when you talk about your dad, and I know you mumble in your sleep, and you love your family business, and you're part of a community that you call home. You know where you belong in this world, and I envy that. I know you're one of the most genuine and sweetest guys I've ever met. And I know I want to see you again. I want to spend more time with you, and I want to know everything there is to know about you. So yeah, we've known each other for 3.5 days, but so what? I know enough to know I want to know more."

My heart was just about thumping right out of my chest and my belly was full of butterflies. Pretty sure my smile told him all he needed to know. "Hamish," I said, trying to catch my breath. "I want more with you too. More of everything. More of you. The last three days have been the best three days I've ever spent with anyone. I can be me with you, and it's so natural and comfortable . . . it feels like I've known you for years. So yeah, when we talked before of possibilities, I mean it. I want to see where things go with us. Because I really like you too. And I think we could have something special. And I know it's complicated. I know you'll be living here, but Mossley's not that far from Hartbridge. And I know you're only here for two years, but honestly, I'll take two years of perfection over a lifetime of mediocre."

He laughed, a little teary. "Perfection? I don't know about that. I mean, it'd be close . . ."

I chuckled, taking in his beautiful smile and those gorgeous dark eyes and how he was carrying Chutney in his coat like a baby. "Haims, I think you could be my Mariah Carey."

He gasped. "Are we David and Patrick from *Schitt's Creek*? Oh my God, we're David and Patrick. I'm David, obviously."

I laughed. "You're possibly more David than the actual David."

He grinned. "Does this mean I can start wearing black skirts over my jeans?"

"If you want." I laughed and nodded back to his sister's house. "How about we go back inside, have some hot coffee, and play a few more games of tic-tac-toe before I have to leave?"

Hamish nodded. "Okay. We should probably check to see if that mistletoe is still there too."

"Ah, tic-tac-mistletoe. That's a game I'd like to play."

He laughed and turned back the way we'd come. "Good, because I can't feel my nose or my feet." We took a few steps. "I am curious, though, how long is kissing under mistletoe a rule for? Like, is it just at Christmas time? Or can we nail it to the ceiling of your bedroom all year round?"

I laughed. "I don't think we'll need it if last night was any indication."

He hummed and he got a wicked gleam in his eye. "That's very true. And you certainly don't need mistletoe to kiss me."

I pulled him to a stop and smacked a kiss square on his lips. "Like that?"

"Well, yes, but I think Chutney would disagree."

We both looked down between us, and sure enough, poor Chutney was a bit squished. She tried to lick me, and I laughed again before taking Hamish's hand again and leading him back to the house.

I didn't think it was that cold—I'd certainly been in colder—but poor Hamish was not used to it. His teeth began to chatter, and he was still chattering and shivering when we got inside. I freed Chutney, took Hamish's coat off, and plonked him on the couch by the fire.

I knelt down at his feet and began to unlace his boots. "Feel okay now?"

"B-better."

"I'll go make some coffee," Liv said before wrapping a throw blanket around his shoulders.

I sat beside him and rubbed his hands. "Maybe a walk wasn't the best idea."

He grinned at me. "It was a great idea." Then he spoke softer. "I didn't want you to leave without sorting a few things out first."

"I'm glad we talked too," I admitted. "Knowing we're on the same page, it makes going home easier."

"It's definitely not a goodbye," he murmured. "But you'll have a busy week after the holiday break, and I have to get sorted out here. I need to buy a new car, find somewhere to rent, probably. Not immediately, but I should start looking." He frowned. "But we can text and call. Or Face-Time if Chutney misses me too much."

"I'm sure she will."

"So next weekend?" He made a face. "That seems so far away."

"I'd like to see you for New Year's," I said, hopeful.

He nodded quickly. "For sure." He cupped my cheek and leaned in for a soft kiss. "I'd like that very much."

He was right, though. It did seem so far away. But if we were an hour and a half apart, then we'd need to learn some patience. And the truth was, I hadn't seen anyone in a lot of months. Surely I could wait a few days between visits.

Liv came back in with two hot coffees, which we took gratefully. "How's the crib building going?" Hamish asked.

She waved her hand. "Easy. And when I say 'easy,' I mean Josh is doing it and he's really good at it, and it took all of ten minutes. He's in there doing the change table now. I better go help." She made a funny face, as if her helping wasn't much help at all, and disappeared down the hall.

Hamish sipped his coffee and hummed, and I rubbed his leg. "Warmer now?"

"Much."

"Still want to play a game?" I nodded at the tic-tac-toe board.

"Sure. You don't think it's . . . silly?"

"Not at all. Actually, I like it. It's significant to you because you played it with your mom. But it's . . . simple and, I don't know, honest, somehow."

"Honest?"

I nodded. "Yeah, like back to basics. I don't know if that's the right phrase. Innocent, maybe. Nice. Genuine. I don't know."

He sighed happily. "I like that."

I grabbed the board from the coffee table and put it on the couch between us. I took the circle pieces and Hamish handed me an X. "You can be the crosses if you want."

"But you're always the crosses."

"I can compromise." He smiled as he collected the O pieces. "Just don't tell anyone."

We played game after game, neither of us keeping score. We ate leftovers for lunch, which were just as good as the night before. We had more cookies for dessert, and all too soon it was time for me to leave.

I threw my bag and the dog's bed into the truck and dashed back up onto the front porch where Hamish was holding Chutney. I'd already said goodbye to Liv and Josh and they'd left me and Hamish alone to say our farewells.

"It's not goodbye," he said again, so confident, so certain. He put his hand to my waist and pulled me close, Chutney wedged safely between us. "I'll see you both again soon. And you have my number and I have yours. Text me when you get home so I know you arrived safely, and I'll call you when I get home from Josh's parents' house after dinner."

I nodded. His surety was heartening, and I pressed my lips to his. "Thank you. For running off the road out the front of my place. For saving me from a miserable Christmas by myself, and for being the best thing to come into my life in a really long time."

He smiled, his eyes soft and twinkling. "I never believed in the magic of Christmas before now," he whispered. "I will see you soon, I promise." He handed Chutney over to me, then took my face in his hands and kissed me properly, lingering and lovely. Then he gave Chutney a gentle pat. "Take care of your daddy for me, and I'll see you both soon."

She licked his palm and I gave him another smiley kiss. "Soon," I murmured, before getting into my truck.

I didn't know exactly when soon would be, but I knew it *would* happen, though it didn't help the heavy heart I drove home with. Even as I pulled up at my house, it was with a sense of melancholy as I went inside.

The house smelled like pine from the Christmas tree, and I smiled at all the Christmas decorations. It had Hamish's touch all over it, even though he was now noticeably absent.

He was here for just three days. How could he have made such an impact? How was it possible for me to miss him so much after just three days? I wasn't sure, but as I looked around my house, I considered taking all the Christmas decorations down but couldn't bring myself to do it.

Instead, I sent him a quick text to let him know I'd arrived safe and sound, and it was nice knowing someone cared, someone that would worry and miss me should something have happened.

I knew he was having Christmas with Liv and Josh's side of the family so I made myself busy cleaning out the fireplace and getting a new fire going. I put a soup on the stove for dinner, then Chutney and I cosied up on the couch when my phone beeped with a message.

Glad you made it. I survived socialising with a houseful of strangers for Christmas dinner, including one moody teenaged niece who didn't get the phone she wanted, a three-legged cat named Hokey Pokey, and a drunk grandpa with a wicked sense of humour.

I laughed out loud as I read it.

Sounds amazing. Dare I ask about the cat?

Probably safer not to. Same with the grandpa. I'm traumatised and currently decompressing in my room pretending to unpack my suitcases.

I chuckled again. *Sounds fair. I'm pretending to watch some terrible movie on TV but I'm really texting some hottie I met three days ago.*

Anyone I know?

Maybe. He's an Aussie guy, darkest brown eyes I've ever see, and a beard that I'm totally into.

Aww.

Oh, and he can't drive in the snow.

Hey!

I laughed again. *But my dog adores him and he makes me happy, and I can't wait to see him again.*

His reply took a second to come through. *Same, Ren. Wish I was there with you right now.*

That made my heart swell and ache at the same time. *Soon, right?*

Promise.

We'd agreed on next weekend, but that felt like a life-time away. I took a selfie of me and Chutney lying on the couch and sent it to him. *Night, Haims.*

Night, Ren xox

I smiled at the xox, being tic-tac-toe and all.

I really missed him. I ached to be with him, to speak to him, to touch him, to hear him laugh. But if this was going to be a long-distance thing, I needed to get used to it. I refused to be sad about it, dwelling on what I was missing, and instead, I focused on the positives.

I'd met someone who made me happy, someone who made me realise I didn't have to settle for loneliness.

And that was a very good feeling.

The next morning, Mrs Barton came into the store bright and early, carrying a stack of containers. I took them for her. "Morning," she said cheerfully. "I brought you in all kinds of leftovers from our Christmas dinner." Before I could argue, she put her hand up. "I can barely close my refrigerator door, there is so much food. Ham, potatoes, apple pie, you name it, we had it." Then she sighed. "Now tell me, how was your day? I worried about you being alone on Christmas Day . . ."

"I, uh . . . I wasn't alone," I began. I briefly contemplated not telling her—I'd never discussed any of my relationships with her—but I was too excited not to tell her. "It's a long story, but it began with a guy running his car off the road in that snowstorm."

"Oh my," she whispered, her hand to her heart.

"He was fine, he wasn't injured or anything, but I took him home. It was snowing pretty hard, we needed to get him out of the cold. He's an Australian guy who'd never driven in snow before."

"And he drove in the snowstorm?"

I nodded. "Anyway, the short version is that his sister lives in Mossley, but his rental car had to be towed, and then Beartrap Road was blocked."

"Oh, that poor man."

"Yep. He stayed with me for a few days and I drove him to his sister's place on Christmas Eve. I spent Christmas with them and came home yesterday afternoon."

"Oh, that sounds lovely," she said, her face all warm and rosy.

"Yeah, he is."

She put her hand on my arm, her face suddenly serious. "Are you . . . ? Oh my word, Reynold. Are you and him . . . ? Does this young man have a name? What does he do for a living? He's from where, did you say?"

I chuckled, relieved and a little embarrassed. "His name is Hamish." I filled her in on the details and I knew damn well my stupid face was telling her more than I was. But I'd never talked about guys with her, or with anyone in Hartbridge, to be honest. It was strange to be doing it now, but it felt so good.

"You like him," she said fondly.

"I do. Which is crazy, right? It's so fast, but he's just . . . he's perfect."

She shook her head and gave me her mom-like tsk sound. "It's not crazy at all. I knew the day I met Mr Barton that he was the one for me. I just knew it. I'll never forget it either. The moment I knew. We were on our first date and he was taking me to the diner when old Mrs Adderly was coming out of the store and the bottom of her grocery bag split, and he rushed to help her. I knew right then. He was wearing a brown jacket and the sunshine made his hair look golden, and that was it. I was sure of it."

I smiled at her memory. "Can I tell you something?"

"Of course you can."

"The day after we met, I was taking him to Robert's to see about his car. We were in my truck and he had Chutney on his lap." I let out a nervous laugh, not sure why I was admitting this to anyone. "But he had my dog on his lap, and she had her front paws on the door, looking out the window, and he was talking to her, pointing out all the things we drove past, and I can't be sure . . . Well, I probably *can* be, but maybe I don't want to say it out loud . . ."

"But you knew."

I nodded. "I think so, yeah."

"He must be special."

I don't know why I got emotional, but just saying this all out loud hit me right in the heart. "I think he could be."

She put her hand on my arm, nodding, a bit teary like me. "Then you take it in both hands and hold it close for as long as you're able." She nodded before composing herself, breathing deep and raising her chin. "I do expect to meet this young man, I hope you know."

I barked out a laugh, blinking away my tears. "I'd like that."

"Good. Now let's put these containers in the fridge and open up the store," she said, all business again.

Of course, she knew I was gay, but this was the first time I'd openly discussed my love life with her, and more specifically me seeing another man, and it felt . . . I couldn't even describe how it felt. Amazing. Renewing. Validating.

I nodded, trying not to grin, feeling happier and lighter than I had since before my dad passed away. Mrs Barton had said to grab a hold of happiness with both hands and don't let go, and I had every intention of doing exactly that.

CHAPTER THIRTEEN

HAMISH

IT HAD BEEN four days since I'd seen Ren. We'd texted a lot, we'd spoken on the phone a lot, and we FaceTimed so Chutney could join in, but it had been four days.

I'd unpacked my clothes, done some laundry, sorted through the boxes I'd shipped over earlier, and even bought a car. Well, it was an SUV-type thing. I was not a ute kind of guy, or a truck as they called them here. Ren's truck suited him because he was basically a lumberjack hardware man. But I was more of a creature-comforts kind of guy, with seat warmers and tinted windows. And a sedan didn't make much sense considering the damned snow. With my inability to drive in it, it was safer to go with something bigger.

Even if the salesman didn't give me a discount for the steering wheel being on the wrong side. It wasn't my fault he didn't have a sense of humour.

I'd been in contact with work and got everything prepared for my first day being fully remote, and I was excited for that to start. I'd even done some googling on places to rent. Nothing had grabbed me so far, and Liv was in no hurry for me to find my own place, but it didn't hurt to start looking.

I'd seen the very short list of sights of Mossley, which was all fine and well. I took Liv out for lunch, we did some shopping, and it was wonderful to spend time with her.

But my God, I missed Ren.

"Just go," Liv said. "Go and see him. Surprise him or tell him. I can see how much you want to."

I sighed, but butterflies swarmed my belly at the mention of seeing him. "I'm sure I can wait another two days. The plan was to go up on Friday and spend the weekend for New Year's."

"Hamish," Liv said gently. She patted my hand and met my eyes. "Go."

I smiled. "Do you think he'd mind?"

"Are you kidding me? Your phone hasn't stopped pinging and you get that dopey look on your face, and honestly, Haims, I'm sure he misses you too."

I was on the road twenty minutes later.

I drove up that bloody mountain slower than molasses on a cold day. Cars honked behind me and I gave them the Australian wave as they overtook me, and it took me two hours instead of the ninety minutes it took Ren.

But I made it.

I drove over that cute little bridge into Hartbridge and it felt like coming home. And that was an emotional response I'd have to unpack and pull apart later, but all I could think about was seeing Ren.

It was mid-afternoon and Main Street was just as pretty as I remembered; covered in snow, quaint shopfronts, smiling people. Christmas decorations still adorned the streetlamps and windows.

I pulled up out the front of Hartbridge Hardware and

managed to reverse parallel park without any major traffic incidents. My belly was in knots, my hands were shaking, but I pulled on my beanie and got out of the car.

A cute bell chimed above the door when I opened it, and I noticed a few things at once. The first was the size of the shop. It was bigger than it looked from the outside. There were rows of nuts and bolts, axes, hammers, safety gear, chains, and a bunch of stuff I couldn't name.

The second thing I noticed was the smell.

It was sawdust and oil, or polish, or something . . . It smelled like Ren.

A lady came over to me. She was in her sixties, maybe, with a round kind face and a pretty smile. "Can I help you?"

"Uh, yes." I tried to think on my feet because I was pretty sure this was Mrs Barton, but I didn't know what Ren had told her exactly and I didn't want to throw him under the rainbow coloured bus. "I need a wheel. A caster wheel for a broken suitcase. I was told you might have them here."

She smiled and tilted her head. She paused for a moment. "You're Australian," she murmured. Then she turned to the back of the shop. "Ren? There's . . ."

Her words trailed off because Ren was walking out. He was carrying some huge box that he slid onto the counter, and he dusted his hands off on his apron, and it was only then he seemed to see me.

I grinned at him. "I heard you can fix a broken suitcase?"

He crossed the floor in three long strides and collected me in a crushing hug. His body, his heat, his smell, his everything just melted away any apprehension I'd had about driving up earlier. "I've missed you," he murmured.

"I missed you too," I squeaked out. "I know it's not Friday, but—"

He kissed me into silence, and too bad if there were other customers—Mrs Barton had somehow disappeared—and when he broke the kiss, he hugged me again. Then Chutney was yapping at my leg, so I picked her up and gave her a cuddle, and Ren pulled on my arm leading me over to the counter.

"Mrs Barton, this is Hamish Kenneally. Hamish, Mrs Barton."

"Nice to meet you," I said, holding a smiling Chutney to my chest.

She was behind the counter, grinning now, teary-eyed. "I can't tell you how long it's been since I've waited to meet you. Not you, in particular," she clarified. "Just someone to make our Ren happy. It's about time."

"Oh," I said, because that wasn't embarrassing at all.

Ren tucked me into his side, where I fit like a puzzle piece. "Mrs Barton," he began.

"Why don't you boys go home," she said, interrupting whatever it was he was about to say. She looked at the clock. "It's closing time soon anyway."

"There's two hours to go," Ren tried.

She raised an eyebrow. "Are you saying I'm not capable?"

"No, of course not. Of course you are—"

"Then it's settled," she said, smiling victoriously. "And yes, the Bixton's are picking up their order at four, and Julie Martinez will be in to measure for her new bathroom cabinetry. I know these things."

Ren sighed, but a smile pulled at his lips. "You're sure?"

She all but rolled her eyes. "Ren, my sweet boy. This is a one-time offer."

He put his hands up. "Okay, okay."

I laughed and handed Chutney back to Ren. "I'll see you at your place."

"You drove your new car up?"

"I did! Very slowly, and I screamed and panicked more than I'd care to admit, but I did."

He planted a smiley kiss on my lips. "I'll follow you."

"Hope your truck likes second gear." He laughed but I wasn't kidding. I turned to Mrs Barton. "It was very nice to meet you."

She gave me that grandmotherly smile and threatened Ren to bring me over for dinner one night before all but ushering us away.

I drove out of town and Ren's truck was soon behind me. I could see him smiling in my rear vision mirror and I tried not to get too excited . . . The last thing I wanted to do was run off the road again. But my belly was in knots by the time I pulled up at his house. I grabbed my bag and Ren and Chutney met me on the porch. "Nice car," he said.

"Thanks."

Ren was still grinning when he unlocked the door, and I only got as far as putting my bag down by the couch when he was on me. His hands cupped my face, his lips found mine, and he pushed me against the back of the couch as he pushed his tongue into my mouth.

Oh, hell fucking yes . . .

I could feel how hard he was already. I could feel the emotions in his touch, in his kiss.

And then he stopped, as if he'd just realised what he'd done. "Sorry, I didn't mean to attack you," he mumbled, heavy-lidded and swollen lipped. "I know we said we'd take it slow."

I licked the corner of my mouth, my breath was ragged,

and every part of me was aching with need. I picked up my bag and took his hand, leading him to the room I'd stayed in. The bed was remade and I upended my bag, the contents spilling onto the covers. Noticeably there was a box of condoms and a large tube of lube. "I thought I'd be prepared, given slow has many variables."

He laughed, low and rumbly, so I pulled him by his shirt so I could kiss him again, and he laid me down on that bed and made short, short work of me. Before long, he was on top of me, inside me, thrusting deep and sure, kissing me, holding me. I felt every shudder of his restraint, every murmur of lips at my throat, my ear. Every pulse, every heartbeat. I felt it all.

He made love to me until every inch of me was wrung out, adored, and boneless. He was tender and gentle and so very thorough. He was everything I knew he would be, and more.

"I never want to leave," I mumbled some hours later. We hadn't moved from the bed, or were *un*able to move was more like it. We'd probably need to think about food at some point, and maybe some water. But God, his arms, his body against mine, his mouth . . .

"Then don't leave," he replied. "After New Year's, stay here. Don't go back to Mossley. Don't find your own place. Stay here with me and Chutney."

I lifted my head up so I could see his face. He was dead serious.

"This house felt empty without you," he added softly. "And now you're here again . . . we could have this." He gestured to us both. "We could have this all the time."

"Ren . . ."

"I know it's more complicated than that," he said, more conviction in his voice now, like he knew what he was saying was the truth. "But what we have is special. When I saw you in my store today, I knew . . ."

"You knew what?"

"That I want to make this work. That I need you in my life. That I'm falling in love with you."

I gasped. My heart skidded to a stop in my chest. "Ren . . ."

He rolled on top of me, his body a delicious weight on mine, and kissed me softly. "I think I knew that the day I met you."

I put my hand to his cheek and scanned the depths of blue in his eyes. "I think I knew too. Well, I questioned my sanity on the matter, but there were definite moments of clarity."

He grinned and closed his eyes, resting his forehead on mine, and when he looked at me again, his eyes were glassy. "Stay."

I nodded and he kissed me again, deep and with every emotion I could now taste between us. It was kinda scary that things had moved so fast, but it also felt right. I was falling in love with him, maybe I was in love with him already and I'd just been too afraid to admit it.

But I *was* going to stay, and that was the rightest I'd felt in years.

EPILOGUE
ONE YEAR LATER

WE'D LOADED everything into my SUV on Christmas Eve, and Ren drove down to Mossley while Chutney and I sat in the passenger side looking at all the pretty scenery.

I'd made this drive dozens of times now but I still preferred it when Ren drove. It was kind of perfect being ninety minutes from Liv. We got to see each other all the time without being in each other's pockets. When baby Stevie was born, I'd stayed to help out with laundry and cooking, or even just baby-ogling while the exhausted new parents caught up on some much-needed sleep.

Stevie was the cutest almost-seven-month old baby to ever exist. And as her uncle, I was completely impartial in this proclamation, of course. They had decided that the name Migaloo, while cute, was not probably appropriate for a newborn girl, so they called her Stevie Kathryn, after Stevie Nicks and my mother, Kathryn Kenneally. Okay, well, they didn't actually name her after Stevie Nicks, but I liked the rock-star vibe. And apparently they didn't name her after Stevie from *Schitt's Creek*, but I wasn't entirely convinced. Not that it mattered, I was happy with either.

But Ren and I made awesome uncles, if I did say so myself. I mean, we were good dads to Chutney, so it was a given, but Ren adored Stevie.

Things between Ren and myself had never been better. I pretty much moved in before New Year's last year and we'd never looked back. We'd only ever had one argument and that was over folding towels. Which, for the record, I do the correct way—folded into thirds—and Ren folded them in half, then half again. Which is clearly wrong and, quite frankly, monstrous. The fact that this argument blew up when I was scrubbing the house from top to bottom while waiting on news of Stevie's birth was beside the point. Actually, it was probably the whole entire point and a valid reason why I was so stressed, and anyway, the short version of our one and only fight story is that now I am in charge of folding all the towels.

"You okay?" Ren asked, sliding his hand onto my thigh.

I held his hand and smiled. "Perfect."

"You seem nervous."

I shot him a look. "Nervous? What would I be nervous about?"

He smiled and shrugged. "Dunno. Christmas will be perfect."

I squeezed his hand. "I know."

Well, I hoped it would be . . .

We arrived and unloaded everything and I got first cuddles with Stevie while Ren drank his coffee; then we swapped. Ren and I had brought a lot of the food we'd made yesterday so all we had to do was reheat it for dinner tonight. There was ham and lamb and vegetables au gratin and a whole bunch of Christmas cookies.

The idea was for us to have Christmas dinner on Christmas Eve, and on Christmas Day, when Liv, Josh, and

Stevie went to spend time with his family, Ren and I would head home. That way we could be home after lunch, spend Christmas night on a makeshift bed on the floor in front of the fire, and Ren wouldn't be rushed to open the store the next day.

And our Christmas Eve dinner was lovely, with Stevie's highchair at the table—her first Christmas. We toasted to family, those here and those who weren't. We watched more awesomely terrible Christmas movies and we had a few eggnogs, and we went to bed with full bellies and fuller hearts. I fell asleep in Ren's arms and he woke up in mine.

"Merry Christmas," I whispered, rubbing his back.

"Hm, Merry Christmas."

"Can you believe it's been one year?" I asked wistfully.

"It's been the best year."

"It has," I replied. I didn't want him to mention that this was our halfway point. My two-year visa was half over. I knew his mind would follow the same steps mine had, and last time I mentioned my visa, he was sad for a week, so I needed to change the subject. "Come on, let's get up. I heard Stevie yammering away already. Pretty sure Santa's been."

I went straight out to the living room, following the smell of coffee and toast. "Morning," I said brightly. "Merry Christmas!"

Ren followed me out, still a little sleepy and probably a little more confused at my quick departure. "Morning," he said, his voice croaking.

I handed him a cup of coffee. "Should we do breakfast first? Or presents?"

"Presents," Liv replied. She knew I was nervous and excited about this, but not wanting to let on, she added, "It's Stevie's first Christmas."

No one had the bad manners to say Stevie had no idea what Christmas even was. She got presents almost every time someone came to visit, but that wasn't the point.

So we sat on the couches and Josh handed out the gifts. He pulled the big box we'd brought with us over first. "This one is to Stevie, from Uncle Hamish and Uncle Ren."

Liv opened it and put her hand to her mouth when she saw what it was. I'd told her Ren was making Stevie something, like he'd made the spinning mobile that hung over her crib with the wooden Australian animals on it. He'd once said his dad had the knack for handcrafting wooden toys, but holy hell, Ren had found a hidden talent. And I think part of him loved doing it because it made him feel close to his dad.

But he'd spent more time on this gift. It was a push walker trolley type thing that had wooden blocks in the front. He'd made it all by hand, added wheels and stabilisers, and made different shaped wooden blocks, and painted each one with non-toxic paint in subtle pinks and whites. It looked like something from a high-end toy store.

It was gorgeous.

And, of course, I'd bought her clothes and shoes and a beautiful plush wombat, but Ren's gift was something special.

There were other gifts between us all, but it was soon my turn to give Ren his present. "We kind of agreed to no expensive gifts and I wanted to do something meaningful. So, it's mostly papers," I said, swallowing hard.

Ren gave me a curious look as he unwrapped it. It was about the size of a manila folder. Okay, it was the exact size of a manila folder, but it was the papers inside of the manila folder that mattered.

Ren frowned when he saw the folder but he opened it, and he read the first page.

US immigrants visa application . . .

His eyes shot to mine. "Haims," he whispered.

"Keep reading," I managed to say.

He scanned the first page and flipped through the next fifty-something pages, then stood up and crushed me in a hug. "You're staying?"

I nodded, unable to stop my tears. "Liv helped me with the application. I can't bear the thought of leaving you, Ren," I said. "I left Australia because nothing felt right, and I came here and met you, and everything just clicked into place."

He hugged me again, lifting my feet off the ground and making my spine crack seven different ways before he put me back down and he hugged me for the longest time. "I love it. I love you. But that makes my gift to you seem kinda lame," he said with a frown.

"No, it won't," I said. He handed me the box and we sat down so I could open it. It was a decent-sized box but it wasn't overly heavy, and I had *no* idea what was in it. I ripped into the wrapping paper and opened it to find . . . lots of felt pouches. "What are these?" I wondered, pulling one out.

I opened the first one, and inside were wooden pieces, shapes, hand painted by the looks of them, about the size of milk bottle lids . . . Six pink hearts and six purple hearts.

"Open this one," he said, handing me another pouch from the box.

These shapes were wooden . . . "Candy canes and mistletoe," I whispered.

"For your tic-tac-toe board," he said, making an embarrassed face. "I did different themed ones so we could play it all year around. He took out another pouch and inside were pumpkins and cauldrons. "These ones are Halloween. The hearts are for Valentine's Day. And there's another one of kangaroos and emus, just because it's for you. And it's not taking anything away from your mom's game, but I know you love it and I thought it'd be fun if we did themes and we could play it all year."

"Ren," I mumbled, teary again. "This is the most beautiful gift I've ever got."

"You like it?" he asked.

"I love it. God, I love it so much. It's perfect." I leaned over and kissed him. "I love you."

He finally smiled. "It's not as good as your gift. I can't believe you're staying. Haims, that's . . . that's the best gift ever. You just made me the happiest man in America."

I picked up a piece of wooden mistletoe. "Now we get to really play tic-tac-mistletoe." I held it above my head and he gave me a smiley kiss.

Then he whispered, "I left one pouch at home. It has peach and eggplant pieces, like the emojis . . ."

I burst out laughing. "I'm the peach, right? You know I will let you win deliberately when we play that."

He grinned and looked over the paperwork for my application to stay in America. "You're really staying?"

"I'm home here," I replied. "With you and Chutney in Hartbridge. It's where I belong."

Ren wiped away a tear and laughed, embarrassed. "Merry Christmas to me." Then he chewed on his lip. "You know what else would let you stay here?" He met my eyes. "If we got married."

Liv gasped, and I put my hand to my mouth, trying not to freak out, but my heart almost exploded in my chest. Ren took one of the pouches and fished out a sparkly rainbow O piece and held it up. "These are the rainbow pieces for Pride month," he said and took my hand. "I honestly hadn't planned to do this, but God, this feels so right. Hamish, will you marry me?"

I nodded, crying, blubbering like David in *Schitt's Creek*, season five, episode thirteen.

You know the one.

Ren slipped the glittery rainbow tic-tac-toe piece onto my ring finger, and he kissed me. A teary, snot-sobbing kiss, and then we were being hugged and cried all over, and it was, without a doubt, the best day of my life.

"Merry Christmas to me," I blubbered.

Ren pulled me against him, kissing the side of my head and holding me tight. "Merry Christmas to us."

The Merry End

ABOUT THE AUTHOR

N.R. Walker is an Australian author, who loves her genre of gay romance. She loves writing and spends far too much time doing it, but wouldn't have it any other way.

She is many things: a mother, a wife, a sister, a writer. She has pretty, pretty boys who live in her head, who don't let her sleep at night unless she gives them life with words.

She likes it when they do dirty, dirty things... but likes it even more when they fall in love.

She used to think having people in her head talking to her was weird, until one day she happened across other writers who told her it was normal.

She's been writing ever since...

ALSO BY N.R. WALKER

The Dichotomy of Angels

Throwing Hearts

Pieces of You - Missing Pieces #1

Pieces of Me - Missing Pieces #2

Pieces of Us - Missing Pieces #3

Lacuna

Titles in Audio:

Cronin's Key

Cronin's Key II

Cronin's Key III

Red Dirt Heart

Red Dirt Heart 2

Red Dirt Heart 3

Red Dirt Heart 4

The Weight Of It All

Switched

Point of No Return

Breaking Point

Starting Point

Spencer Cohen Book One

Spencer Cohen Book Two

Spencer Cohen Book Three

Yanni's Story

On Davis Row

Free Reads:

Learning to Feel

His Grandfather's Watch (And The Story of Billy and Hale)

The Twelfth of Never (Blind Faith 3.5)

Twelve Days of Christmas (Sixty Five Hours Christmas)

Best of Both Worlds

Translated Titles:

Fiducia Cieca (Italian translation of Blind Faith)

Attraverso Questi Occhi (Italian translation of Through These Eyes)

Preso alla Sprovvista (Italian translation of Blindside)

Il giorno del Mai (Italian translation of Blind Faith 3.5)

Cuore di Terra Rossa (Italian translation of Red Dirt Heart)

Cuore di Terra Rossa 2 (Italian translation of Red Dirt Heart 2)

Cuore di Terra Rossa 3 (Italian translation of Red Dirt Heart 3)

Cuore di Terra Rossa 4 (Italian translation of Red Dirt Heart 4)

Natale di terra rossa (Red dirt Christmas)

Intervento di Retrofit (Italian translation of Elements of Retrofit)

A Chiare Linee (Italian translation of Clarity of Lines)

Senso D'appartenenza (Italian translation of Sense of Place)

Spencer Cohen 1 Serie: Spencer Cohen

Spencer Cohen 2 Serie: Spencer Cohen

Spencer Cohen 3 Serie: Spencer Cohen

Spencer Cohen 4 Serie: Yanni's Story

Punto di non Ritorno (Italian translation of Point of No Return)

Weil Leibe uns immer Bliebt (German translation of Switched)

Drei Herzen eine Leibe (German translation of Three's Company)

Sixty Five Hours (Thai translation)

Finders Keepers (Thai translation)

CPSIA information can be obtained
at www.ICGtesting.com
Printed in the USA
LVHW031758260121
677549LV00005B/771